Carelessness of

the Heart

An Urban Fiction Tale

D1569344

Carelessness of

the Heart

An Urban Fiction Tale

Tasha Wright

Passionate Writer Publishing

Indiana and Georgia

Passionate Writer Publishing

www.passionatewriterpublishing.com

This book is a work of fiction. Names, characters, places, and incidents
either are products of the author's imagination or are used fictitiously.
Any resemblance to actual events or locales or persons, living or dead,
is entirely coincidental.

©2012 Tasha Wright

ISBN 13

First Edition

10 9 8 7 6 5 4 3 2 1

Manufactured in the United States of America.

Passionate Writer Publishing can bring authors to your live event. For
more information or to book an event, contact Passionate Writer
Publishing at www.passionatewriterpublishing.com.

Also by Tasha Wright

When a Tattered Past Catches You
2010

Dedication

I would like to thank my savior Jesus Christ for my creative gift of writing. This book is dedicated to my grandfather Johnnie O. Henderson. I hope I make you proud every day. I love you more than I could ever express in words. I would also like to thank all my family and friends. Mainly, my mother Lillie Scott, my dad Larry Wright, and my grandmother Lillie Henderson. I would also like to share this with my two brothers Shannon and DeRoyce Wright. We can make anything possible between the three of us! Never stop. I hope you all enjoy this book because it is my first creation enhanced!

A special thank you to Passionate Writer Publishing…Dreams do come true with hard work, patience, and a great team! You guys as AWESOME and thank you for believing in me!

Chapter One

The sunlight shining through the white blinds awakened Carrie. Stretching her long body, she relaxed in bed until the ringing phone demanded her attention. She had no need to look at her caller ID since the call was so early in the morning. It could only be one person. Letting out a groan, she rolled over and picked up the phone. "Hello, Ronald."

"I love it when you know it's me calling," he laughed.

Carrie glanced at her digital clock. "I don't see anything funny. It's eight o'clock in the morning. Why are you calling so early? As a matter of fact, why do you keep calling when you know it bugs me?"

Ronald ignored her complaints. "Let's get together and do something today."

"You and I will never happen. Please, just stop calling me." She hung up the cordless phone and grabbed her day planner to ensure her day was totally free. Carrie needed to forget about Ronald and his antics. Her best friend Janitta was the remedy for that. It took her all of one hour to get dressed, jump into her car, and lower every window. Swerving around the curved interstate as the wind blew threw her long, curly hair, she became a road warrior. Carrie zipped through the quiet neighborhood until she reached Janitta's house. She looked into her mirror and combed her hair from her ride of freedom.

"Hi, my name is Terrence Coleman. And you are?" said a tall gentleman standing by her door.

"Hello. My name is Carrie." She smiled. This tall mysterious man had smooth dark skin and anyone could tell he took pride in his appearance. His hair was cut very low in a taper fade. "I'm a little confused. I'm a friend of Janitta's and I have never heard her mention you before." Carrie proceeded to turn off her engine and step out her car.

Terrence revealed a perfect smile. "I'm here with Ronald. He's inside with Janitta."

Carrie's smile quickly turned to a frown. He had to have a few screws loose to be friends with Ronald. "Wow. How do you know him?"

"We work together. Is he your boyfriend?"

"God, no; Ronald is what you would call an aggressively annoying person."

"I hope that doesn't reflect negatively on me. If you don't mind me saying so, I find you very attractive."

"That depends. Are you anything like your friend in there?"

Terrence laughed. "I can't honestly answer that question. I don't know what it is about Ronald that makes your blood boil. However, I know this may be too forward, but how would you like to accompany me to a play tonight? I have two tickets and no one to share them with. It would give you a chance to find out for yourself if I'm anything like Ronald."

"I don't know about that." She held her head down. "I don't know if I could handle another Ronald in my life."

Terrence retrieved a small business card from his black wallet. "Come on. I know you wouldn't deny yourself the chance to get to know me because of the company I keep. He can't be that bad."

"You have no idea, but I'm going to take a chance and trust you this one time. My address is 1221 North Conrad Avenue," she replied. "Don't let me down."

Terrence jotted the address down. "We live really close. You're about five minutes from me."

"Is that so? Now if you don't mind I have some place to be and you are blocking the door."

He flashed a grin, allowing her entry into Janitta's modest brick home as he followed closely behind.

"Good morning, J. How are you doing, darling?" Carrie embraced her friend.

"I'm fine, but not as good as you." Janitta pointed at Terrence. "So what are you up to besides meeting and greeting?"

"Well, you know whenever I have time I have to check on my dearest friend."

Ronald stood. "Hey man, I saw you outside. It looked like you were trying to come on to my girl."

"I don't mean any disrespect in saying this, Ronald, but from what I was told, she was never your woman," Terrence replied.

"So, you're a comedian now?"

"I'm not being sarcastic. I think she's a very nice lady so I asked her on a date."

Ronald stood in front of Carrie. "You're going on a date with someone you just met, but yet you won't take the time to get to know me and we've known each other for a while now?"

"Please stop with this same old act. You're not my type." Carrie brushed Ronald away.

He pointed at Terrence. "I guess this is your type."

"I'd really like to enjoy my day." She took a seat and crossed her legs.

"No problem. But you will hear from me soon. Remember this day." Ronald sat beside Janitta.

Carrie rolled her eyes. "Terrence, what time should I be ready tonight?"

"Seven o'clock, straight up. It was very nice to meet you, Janitta. I will see you later, Sexy." Carrie blushed. "I'll see you tonight." Mesmerized, she watched Terrence walk away.

Ronald stood and eased over to Carrie as he spoke, "You know this isn't right, Carrie."

"You're not my type. Terrence, on the other hand, is something worth exploring."

"What does he have that I don't," Ronald asked.

"He didn't approach me the way you did." She poked her chest out like a macho man, mimicking Ronald. "What's up with you and me? How can I be down?"

"I'm a real man," he responded, pounding his bony chest. "I wasn't trying to beat around the bush. He's just trying to get you at the right time to sleep with you."

"That was a very ignorant comment, Ronald. Not every man thinks the same warped way you do. Now, to close this conversation, *I* choose who I want to be with, not you." She rolled her eyes again.

Janitta clapped in laughter. "Just give it up, Ronald. She doesn't want to be with you. She never has."

He grabbed his cell phone from the end table. "Look, I'll talk to you ladies another time." He stormed out of the house.

"He really needs to learn a better way to approach a real woman. If he continues to act the way he has with me with other women, that man will forever be alone. I don't know why you even entertain him. He's clearly demented," Carrie rambled.

"Okay, okay, forget about Ronald." Janitta adjusted herself in the seat. "Fill me in on all the details with you and Terrence."

"What details? What do you mean?"

"Oh, don't play with me. Spill the details girl." Janitta playfully hit Carrie's shoulder. "You know what I'm talking about."

"There's nothing to tell. Terrence and I had a great conversation and we're going out tonight."

"Oh really? Where are you going?"

"He said he had tickets to a play. But, let's not forget he's associated with Ronald, so I'll be taking my stun gun with me."

Janitta laughed before speaking. "You're something else. You'll never change."

"I have to be real about this. I don't want to become a victim tonight."

"I'm so jealous of you right now. Terrence is a very suave man."

"If you think he's all that, why didn't you try to talk to him?"

"I guess it's safe to say he's not attracted to big women."

"Did you buy a couple new toys or do you have visitors?" Carrie asked ignoring Janitta's down play of her self-worth.

"Oh, God no; my niece and nephew are here with a few friends. They're outside swimming."

"Times have surely changed. When I was their age, I was still a passenger wishing I could own something that required gasoline. I remember when my friend Jason and I used to sneak out in his mother's car. When we got busted I think I was on punishment for the remainder of my teenage life."

"Girl, you're crazy. My parents would've killed me." They both giggled and high-fived at the statement. "By the way how are your mom and dad doing after everything that's happened with your dad's health?"

"Dad's actually doing much better. You know Nurse Maurine wouldn't have it any other way. My mom's always been a nurturer so taking care of dad is right up her alley."

"I still can't believe your dad had a stroke. I'm praying for his recovery."

"That's why you're my BFF." Carrie smiled. "I just talked to him the other day and he was complaining about Aunt Jackie."

"My goodness; is she still hanging around them every day?"

"Of course, but I don't understand why she's spending so much time over there? But enough about them; what are you doing tonight? Any special plans?"

"What else would I be doing besides sitting in this empty house waiting on that man of mine?" Janitta answered.

"Why do you stay with William? Every time you say his name you frown. I can actually see your happiness drain away."

"I love him, I guess."

"You guess. If you're so unsure about William, maybe you need to reevaluate your relationship." Carrie looked at her diamond-clustered watch. "Goodness, time flies when you're not being stalked. I need to get home so I can get myself ready for my date tonight."

Janitta hugged her friend as she walked Carrie to the door. "Call me as soon as you get home tonight. I don't care what time it is. I want to make sure you make it home safely."

"Will do."

Chapter Two

Maurine moved away from the chatter to answer her ringing phone. "Carrie is that you, baby? How are you doing? We were just talking about you."

"Who's there mom and was the conversation you were having about me good or bad?" she asked.

"Jackie is in the other room with your father, Reshay, and Stephanie are in here with me. You know those two are bickering as always. I swear, you would think they were sisters instead of cousins the way they carry on with one another. We were talking about how you let a good man slip through your fingers. I'm going to tell you once again. You're not getting any younger."

"Mom, please don't do this today. Davion made his decision. I know you just want me to be happy, but enough is enough. It's been a year now. He's gone, Mom."

Maurine shook her head. "Honey, I have a houseful and I need to check on your dad. I'm sure he's tired of Jackie talking his ear off. I'll call you about this later, sweetheart." Walking into the living room, she placed the phone down. "Stephanie and Reshay, how are you girls setting a good example for the kids by acting like silly adolescents? Hush up with all this bickering."

"Auntie, I love you, but how in the world did you manage give birth to someone so evil? Stephanie you have always been so bossy, but I'm not the same little kid you've always pushed around. You need to understand that and respect the woman I am."

Stephanie jumped up from the black stool. "Evil?" she repeated. "You have some nerve."

Reshay stood from the sofa and paced toward the door. "I need to get out of here. Mom, are you coming with me," she called out.

Jackie poked her head out of the family room. "Honey, I'm going to stay a while longer and help out with Jimmie."

Maurine squinted her eyes and headed into the room and held Jimmie's hand. "Thank you, sister, for all your help, but I can take care of my husband from here."

"I said I'm staying. Now, no need to thank me. That's what family is for," Jackie replied, and retreated to the bathroom.

"What the heck is going on with her?" Stephanie whispered. "Jackie's up to something. Why does she care about dad all of a sudden?"

"Auntie, I think I better get out of here before this evil troll pisses me off more than she already has. Why is it so wrong for someone to care?" Reshay rolled her eyes and headed in a beeline towards the door.

Stephanie followed Reshay yapping away, "All of you AKA sorority females are just alike. You walk around with your noses turned up at everyone as if you're better than the next person."

"Boy was I wrong about you. I never thought your attitude could get any worse than it always has been but dang if you hadn't surprised me."

Stephanie smirked. "The only person with an attitude is you." She backed off to join her mother and father in the other room.

Jackie placed her hand on Stephanie's arm "What is your problem? Why do I have to be questioned every time I try to help out around here?"

"I'm going to ask you only once to take your hands off of me. You of all people know I do not like for anyone to touch me," Stephanie said in a calm tone.

Jimmie snatched his blanket and tossed it onto the floor. "Hey, what's going on here? I can't rest with everyone at each other's throat. If you guys want me up, I'm up. Are you happy now?"

Maurine placed the blanket back over her husband and replied, "Honey, it's just Stephanie and Jackie. You know how they get when they are around each other for too long. Don't get yourself all worked up."

Jackie snapped out of her fixation on Stephanie and ran over to Jimmie. "Do you need anything? Is there anything I can do for you? I apologize for that. We shouldn't be adding any stress on you in your condition."

Jimmie pulled his arm away from Jackie's grip. "I think it would be best for you to leave. I'm not in the mood to hear you guys fussing and fighting."

"No, no, we're just fine." Jackie placed a pillow behind Jimmie's back for comfort.

"Thank you, but could you step out for a minute because I need to talk to Maurine alone?"

"Sure. Stephanie, why don't you come with me?" Jackie motioned for Stephanie to follow her out and she obliged.

"Jimmie, don't say a word. I don't know what's going on with Jackie. Maybe she just wants to help out. I'll have a talk with her." Maurine explained.

"No, she's okay. I want you to talk to Stephanie. She's been way over the top lately, even for her."

"I will. Rest assured honey." Maurine replied. She went in search of Jackie down the long narrow hallway, where she found Jackie and Stephanie bickering. "Stephanie, go talk to your father please. Now, Jackie are you going to talk to me about what's going on with you? Why have you been fussing over Jimmie so much lately?"

"What in the world are you talking about," Jackie asked placing the pillow in her lap.

"Jackie, you're my sister. You can't lie to me without me knowing you're lying. Your eyes get all squinty. You and Jimmie have never gotten along, so why are you taking so much interest in him? To be honest you would have been the last person I expected to be at his beck and call. So, I'm going to ask you again. What is going on with you?"

"Why is everyone making such a big deal out of this? We're family. Aren't we supposed to look out for one another?"

"I'm not going to argue with you about this anymore. I just wanted to know where the sudden interest was coming from. I think you should go home and get some rest. I'll take it from here."

Jackie stood from the beige sofa and gathered her things. "I'll just let Jimmie know I'm leaving."

Stephanie slowly entered the room and whispered as she watched Jackie disappear down the hall. "Mom, seriously; this has my curiosity in major overload so I know you have to wondering what the heck is going on with her."

"Oh, I'm very curious, I have tons of patience. Shady business done in the dark always finds its way to light. I just don't know if I'm ready to learn exactly what that truth could be with the two of them because I don't know exactly where this sudden relationship is coming from."

Stephanie nodded. "I agree mom."

"Honey, I'm sure it's harmless. I don't want to jump to any conclusions about anything."

"Mom, I know dad and I'm sure there's nothing to worry about. Jackie's just being Jackie—an overbearing control freak." Stephanie heard Jackie's car door slam shut. "When did she start leaving out the backdoor? I'm telling you mom, something is not right here."

"I know you love your father and don't get me wrong, I love him too. But, I agree with you honey. There are some things going on that just don't add up but I don't want to get into this with you. I don't care how old you girls get; I would never put these types of problems on your shoulders."

Jimmie stood around the corner, resting his head against the wall. He'd heard every concern Maurine had, but never uttered a word.

Chapter Three

Carrie shook off the conversation she'd had with her mother. Although she tried very hard, it seemed there was no escaping Davion. Finally arriving home from her visit with Janitta and a day of shopping, Carrie noticed she had limited time to get herself ready for her big date. She searched through her abundance of clothing in her large walk-in closet until she came across a red jumpsuit with a red sheer duster. She'd never had a reason to wear it, but the outfit was sure to hold Terrence's attention on their date. Showered and dressed, she lightly sprayed on her Burberry cologne. Her doorbell rang and she ran to answer it. "You're on time. I love that in a man." She embraced Terrence.

"Wow, you're so beautiful. You look like a sexy brown goddess. Shall I go on," Terrence asked.

Carrie grinned. "You're not so bad yourself, handsome. So, give me the details about our date tonight."

"We're going to the Complex Theatre and after the play I made reservations for us at the finest restaurant in town." Terrence escorted his date to his awaiting truck. Anything on the truck that used to be factory was now chrome and leather. Carrie shook her head and thought *men and their trucks.*

"How exciting. What's the name of this restaurant you seem to think is the finest. I'll see if I agree with you on that," she giggled.

"Well, for personal reasons I feel this is the finest restaurant. But, I'm taking you to Italian Dining," he replied.

Carrie eased inside Terrence's roomy truck as he held the door open. "I'm impressed. How did you manage to get reservations on such short notice? Every time I've tried to attempt making a reservation at that restaurant I've never been successful."

"My dad and I own it. This restaurant is my first love."

"You can't be serious. The owner is Italian. I've seen him before."

"I guess that's why I'm half Italian and half African American. I've never met anyone who couldn't tell by looking at me."

Carrie laughed, "I just thought you had curly hair with a light complexion."

"No sweetheart, that's not the case." He signaled to make a right turn to reach their destination.

Carrie smiled. "That's actually kind of sexy. So, what's the name of the play?"

"*Love's Stories.*" He parked and rushed to the passenger side to open the door for his lovely companion.

"So, you're a romantic?" Carrie stepped out placing her clutch under her arm.

"I strongly believe in love. Don't you?"

"I believe in love, but I refuse to give one hundred percent when my mate is only giving thirty." Carrie shrugged.

"Your comment implies that you've had a rocky past in the relationship department." Terrence observed holding the door open for Carrie to enter the crowded theatre.

"If you've never had your heart broken, then that tells me you're the heart breaker."

"No, No," Terrence repeated. "I'm not a heartbreaker. But, so far I can't see why any man would do that to you. Of course, I'm just getting to know you. You could be the total opposite of what you're showing me right now."

"Some people just don't realize what they have until it's gone." She swallowed the lump in her throat. The conversation had resurrected thoughts of her most recent break-up. She and Davion were engaged over a year ago, but he gave an uncompromising ultimatum for her to move out of state with him or live her life without him.

"You can say that again. I'm a living witness to that. When it's all said and done, that's when people want to try to salvage what they had with you. By then, it's too late."

"Is this your hometown?"

Terrence beamed with pride. "Yes, born and raised. What about you?"

"Washington."

"Not that I'm complaining, but what brought you here?"

"That's easy; a six-figure salary."

"Check you out, big time." Terrence laughed.

"Do you have any children?"

"No, I don't." he looked away.

"I apologize if children are a sore subject for you." She followed Terrence to their seats.

"No, I'm fine."

"Okay, it just seemed as though I hit a soft spot."

"No, totally fine. The play is starting." He pointed.

***

After the play Terrence chauffeured his lovely date to the restaurant in order to make it on time to their dinner reservations. "That play was so emotional. My goodness it brought out feelings I thought I buried a long time ago," Carrie confessed.

Terrence nodded. "Yeah, I didn't know it was going to be that deep for a first date. Oh, hey I never asked you what you did for a living."

"My friend and I are partners at our firm. Maybe you've heard of us at The Johnson and Bates Law Firm."

He snapped his fingers. "Carrie Johnson. I never put two and two together. That's the most powerful law firm in the state. You're a big deal. Damn, that's sexy as hell."

Carrie smiled. "Don't make me blush. The work is stressful, but it's rewarding. Whoever I decide to share my life with will have to understand my work demands a lot of my time. I'm committed to my firm."

Terrence eased his truck into the valet area. "Well, if the man you decide to share your life with can't understand your work is demanding, then you don't need him." He tossed the valet his keys and escorted Carrie into the restaurant where the hostess quickly seated the couple at their reserved table.

"I'm starting to believe your story as being an owner with these perks you have around here," she laughed.

"Oh, dang, you're starting to believe me. Well, I hope you don't mind this table I reserved for us. I thought you may like the view of the water."

"Oh that's totally fine with me. I want to ask you a question about something you told me when we first met. You said that you and Ronald work for the same company. Where is that," Carrie asked.

"I'm on the executive board of the Parkland Heights Hospital."

The waiter set up an ice tray on a silver stand and placed two bottles of champagne inside. "Executive board? I'm impressed. What's with the two bottles of champagne Mr. Fine Restaurant owner?"

Terrence filled both flutes with champagne. "I thought if we had two bottles it would limit the interruptions of the waiter. As far as my occupation, I'd like to think it's impressive. However my mother doesn't think anything I do is notable unless I decide to use my doctoral degree."

"You have your doctoral? You're full of surprises. Tell me more," Carrie asked.

"I studied the wonderful science of Neuropsychiatry."

"The Science of Mental Disorders. I've always found that to be interesting."

"I agree, but it's not something I could see myself doing on a daily basis. Listening and dealing with crazy issues day in and day out."

A tall waiter interrupting the chatty couple's conversation asked, "Have you two decided on what you'd like to order?"

"Just a second. We have a new dish and I'm dying to find out what someone thinks about it. Would you like to try it," Terrence asked.

"Go for it." Carrie sipped her champagne and admired Terrence's smooth skin.

He noticed Carrie gazing at him with a blank stare. "Am I that boring or do you zone out a lot?"

"Wow, no you're not boring me. I was literally admiring how handsome you are," Carrie replied sipping her wine.

"Thanks. So, you asked me about children. Do you ever plan on being a mother someday," Terrence asked moving his hands out of the way to allow the waiter to place their food on the table.

"I'd like to have children eventually. Right now there are a few things I'd like to accomplish before I step into the role of motherhood."

"I see someone has their priorities together."

"I'm doing the best I can to keep my goals as one of my main priorities. Hey, this is really good. Was this your idea," Carrie asked taking a bite.

"I'd like to take all the credit but my dad is the mastermind behind the menu."

"Well, you're dad is a genius. I would love to take cooking lessons from him one day if that's possible."

"That would be right up his alley. He's always trying to find ways to teach anybody who will listen," Terrence laughed and scraped the last of his food onto his fork.

"You don't play when you eat, do you," Carrie asked.

Terrence smiled. "I did eat pretty fast huh? I was so caught up with our conversation. It's something about you that makes me feel at ease. I feel like it's okay for me to be myself around you."

"That makes me feel good to hear you say that because I feel the same way." Carrie pushed her plate away. "I can't eat another bite."

"Oh, you don't have to do the lady like thing and leave food on your plate. You know you want to eat the rest," Terrence laughed.

"No, seriously. I'm so stuffed. I'll have to run an extra mile in the morning."

Terrence motioned for the waiter. "I'll have this packed up so you can enjoy it tomorrow—can't let good food go to waste."

"You are something else." Carrie smiled.

Terrence exhaled and glanced at his watch. "Look at that. It's already midnight." He stood to help Carrie out of her chair and they headed out the restaurant.

"They say time flies when you're having fun."

"Do you have an early day tomorrow," Terrence asked as they waited on the valet to bring his truck.

"Oh no, Sunday is my day to rest. I usually go to church but this week has been so crazy I thought it would be nice to just kick back and not battle with the traffic for one day."

"Yeah, sometimes you owe it to your body and mind to relax. Oh, here's the truck. Let's get out of here."

"I haven't had this much fun in a really long time. Thank you."

"It was definitely my pleasure. Maybe we should take a different route home. You know how rowdy those Saturday night partiers drive."

"I couldn't agree with you more. This highway is a death trap on Saturday nights. Every weekend there is a wreck. When will they learn."

"So, Ms. Carrie, when do you think we could do this again?"

"Oh my gosh, I was waiting for you to ask me out again before we parted ways. Oh, hey look, this is the park I run in. Maybe one day soon we could jog together."

"This is the second time you've mentioned jogging. Are you a fitness junkie," he asked playfully.

"No, I'm far from a fitness nut. Jogging relaxes me and I thought it would be a good way for us to spend a little more time together."

Terrence parked and walked to the passenger side of the truck. "We could make that happen. I was just giving you a hard time."

Carrie took a deep breath. "Thank you again for a great night. How about you come over in the morning and have a cup of coffee with me." They stood on her long porch.

"I would like that very much. Sweet dreams, sweet stuff. I'll see you tomorrow." He placed a gentle kiss on her cheek.

"That was sweet. Good night, Terrence Coleman." Her eyes beamed.

Carrie stood in her window with the phone in her hand and watched him walk back to his truck and disappeared. She grabbed the phone to make good on her word to let Janitta know she was safely at home.

"Hello," Janitta answered.

"I can't believe you're asleep. You're supposed to be the night owl."

"Girl, I'm getting old. How was your date?" Janitta asked.

"To be honest, I can't help but to compare Terrence to Davion. They are so freaking similar in so many ways that it's blowing my mind."

"If you're comparing Terrence to Davion then you better watch out. That man is going to have your nose wide open," Janitta replied.

"That's exactly what I'm afraid of J. But, go back to sleep. I just wanted you to know I made it home. I'm beat and you know I need at least seven hours of sleep or I'm hell on wheels."

Chapter Four

Carrie was sleeping like a baby until the alarm clock blared waking her. She smiled because she knew that alarm meant Terrence would be over soon. Carrie yawned and stretched her long arms out and tugged on her oversized sweatshirt. She walked over to her tall armoire and dressed in a pair of gray spandex tights. Walking downstairs to put on a fresh brew of coffee, Carrie was interrupted by her ringing phone. Ronald's name showed on the caller ID. "Ronald, what do you want?"

"How was your little date last night," he huffed.

"It's way too early in the morning for this. What's your problem?"

"I'm tired of playing these games with you. If I want you, I'll have you and no one or nothing could stop me."

"Who in the hell do you think you are? I can't believe you are taking things this far." Carrie jumped at the sound of someone pounding on her door. She peeked out the window and saw it was Ronald. "Get the hell away from here!" she screamed.

"I'm giving you until the count of three to open this door."

"Get the hell away from here Ronald." She ended his call and desperately began dialing 911. Ronald barged into the house, snatching the phone away from her. He threw it into the wall, shattering it and pinning her down.

"I'm tired of this cat and mouse game with you. I'm a freaking catch. You should want to be with me." He fought to pull her tights off. "You walk around in your tight ass clothes, and then you put me down for wanting to have sex with you." Ronald grabbed Carrie's neck and threw her against the wall. She struggled but she was no match for his size. "If you don't want to give me a chance, I'll *take* it." He thrust himself inside of her.

Carrie screamed from the forced entry and wrestled with Ronald to break free, but the more she resisted, the tighter his grip became. "Please don't do this," she cried. Carrie scratched and pounded his face as hard as she could but none of her actions could stop him.

"Shut the hell up," Ronald ordered.

"Help, help, please," Carrie screamed. "Help, someone help me."

Terrence rushed into the house and snatched Ronald away from Carrie. "What the hell are you doing man?" He roared and pounded Ronald until his fist turned red.

Carrie hurried to call the police. She held back vomiting at the thought of what had just happened and what more would have happened if Terrence not shown up. She did the best she could to pull herself together and dress in her ripped clothes to cover as much as she could.

"You sick bastard." Terrence screamed.

"This has nothing to do with you," Ronald responded fighting to free himself from Terrence's grip.

"How could you stoop so low and do something this sick?"

"I don't think you can handle what's going to go down if you stick your nose into this."

"Shut the hell up you sick ass bastard. Carrie are you okay? I can hear the police sirens."

"I can't…I can't think," she stuttered. "I can't get myself together. I mean, I can't stop shaking."

"Everything's going to be fine. I know it's hard but try to pull yourself together. The police will handle things," Terrence reassured her.

"He's over there!" Carrie screamed to the group of officers entering the house from the door Terrance left open.

An officer asked, "Are you the woman who called?"

"Yes," she nodded with tears flowing pouring her face.

"Are you okay?" One of the officers asked.

"No, can't you see I've been raped."

Another officer reached out to Ronnie on the floor. "It's okay sir. You can let him go now. Stand up and place your hands behind your back."

Terrence rushed to Carrie. "Come on, I'll drive you to the hospital."

"Sir, we have to get her statement."

"You can get it at the hospital," Terrence retorted as he led Carrie out the door.

Ronald reached for the gun strapped to his ankle "You think I'm going to let you do this to me." He aimed the gun at Carrie and pulled the trigger, but Terrence shielded her.

"You *shot* me." Terrence held his stomach and fell to the floor. Carrie placed her hand over the wound to try to stop the bleeding but nothing she did would help.

"Ronald, what have you done," Carrie screamed. Her entire body was shaking from the fear of Terrence's possible demise.

"*Carrie, Carrie*, please *do* something," Terrence moaned. He struggled to try and position himself off his wound to reduce the pain.

An officer quickly rushed over. "No, please sir, try not to move so much. You could make things worse than they are if that bullet moves."

The officers detained Ronald. "The ambulance was only minutes behind us. They should be here any second. I'll get the status now."

"Oh, my God, an ambulance could take too long. He could *die*. I'll take him myself." Carrie tried to help Terrence up from the floor.

The officer grabbed Carrie's hand. "Ma'am I'm serious if you move him that bullet could move and he could die. I hear the ambulance sirens, so please don't touch him."

Carrie stepped away as the emergency workers flooded the house. "Please help him," she begged.

They ran to Terrence with a long stretcher. "Here we go. Lift on three. One, two, three," the sandy-haired man ordered.

"Get a 2 ml IV started. Sir, what is your name?" The man shined the light in Terrence's eyes only to get no reply.

"Thomas, come here. Continue to check his reflexes and pulse rate. If he doesn't respond we could be dealing with paralysis. It's very early to tell these things but they are a factor at this point. Make sure his pupils don't dilate, we don't want to lose him. Do all that you can. Come on, guys, we have to get him to the hospital. Let's move." They rushed out to the ambulance.

"If you plan on riding in the ambulance with him, you should jump in now."

Carrie ran alongside of the EMT team in order to be there for Terrence as he was just there for her.

***

The ambulance arrived at the emergency entrance less than five minutes after leaving Carrie's home. The EMT ran inside quickly listing details to the awaiting physicians and nurses. "We have one black male suffering from a gunshot wound to his left abdomen. He has a 2 ml IV with packing in his left side. We have irrigated the wound. We also have a black female who was raped and she needs to be examined."

"Hey, wait, I'm going with him." Carrie ran alongside the medical staff.

The nurse placed her arm around Carrie. "Come with me. The doctor will take care of him and you need to come with me so we can take care of you as well."

Carrie's eyes filled with tears. "Is he going to be okay?"

The nurse shook her head. "He's in good hands. Doctor Sienna Reese is the head of the emergency department. He has a stable heartbeat and pulse rate. They'll do everything they can for him. Now, please come with me." The nurse placed one hand on Carrie's shoulder.

"Could someone please keep me updated on how he's doing?"

"That won't be a problem. Please, come." The nurse led her to an empty examination room and handed Carrie a hospital gown. "Please take your clothes off and put this on so the doctor can perform his examination. I'll give you a few minutes to change and I'll return with the doctor."

"Wait a minute; I have another question for you."

The nurse stopped in mid track. "Sure, but we have to be mindful of the doctor's time."

"I've never been through anything like this. What type of exam is the doctor going to do?" Carrie asked.

"Well, it will consist of extragenital injury, genital injury, STD's, and also a pregnancy test. However, those things are all on the surface and physical. We always ask that our patients get psychological counseling," the nurse explained.

"Thank you, I'll change now."

The nurse turned to exit the room. "Don't worry, everything will be fine, I'm sure."

Carrie nodded. She hurried to remove her clothes and dress in the hospital gown. "How in the world could Ronald do something like this?" she whispered to herself. She folded her torn clothes and climbed onto the bulky exam table. It took only a few minutes for the nurse and doctor to enter the room.

The doctor smiled. "Hello, I'm Doctor James Edwin. I would shake your hand but I just sterilized. Please lie back and place your feet into the silver stirrups. You will feel a bit of pressure from the speculum."

"Carrie cringed. "Oh, ouch, that's more than a bit of pressure doctor."

"I apologize." He continued his exam as the nurse stood behind a silver table with many medical supplies. She passed the doctor each item as he moved through his exam.

The doctor passed the last item to the nurse for testing. "Here were are. You did great. You can get dressed now. Thank you for bearing with me. I'm truly sorry you had to go through something like this and I really wish you the best."

Carrie smiled. "Thank you. Um, is there any word on how Terrence is doing?"

"I'll tell you what. You get dressed and by the time the nurse returns with your paperwork we will have an update for you," the doctor replied.

"Thank you." Carrie stood from the examination bed to get dressed.

"How about you dress in this since your clothes were torn." The nurse handed Carrie a pair of green scrubs.

"Thank you so much." She obliged.

***

Carrie was lead to the emergency waiting room to wait for Terrence to be transferred to a regular patient room. She found a comfortable spot in her chair and dosed off for what seemed all of ten minutes when she was awoken by the chatting couple sitting next to her. Carrie looked at her watch when she was approached by a doctor still dressed in her green surgery scrubs with the hat and all its trimmings.

"Ms. Johnson, may I speak with you?" The doctor asked.

"Oh yes, how is Terrence?"

The doctor scrolled through his notes on his wireless tablet. "Terrence is a real fighter. He needed surgery to repair the damage the bullet caused. The damages were minimal and he should be better in no time. You'll be able to receive more detailed information from the nurse once he's settled in his room. We are going to move him to room 503 soon."

Carrie exhaled. "Thank you, Doctor. I appreciate you keeping me in the loop with all of the details."

"Not a problem. We do need you to sign paperwork with the receptionist, and then you can go and wait for him in the emergency surgery waiting area."

Carrie nodded as she walked away to speak with the receptionist. "May I help you?" she asked.

"Hello, I need to sign paperwork for Terrence Coleman."

"Oh, yes." The receptionist gathered all the documents and marked each spot. "Here you are."

Carrie signed the stack of papers. "Is there anything else I need to do? I really need to go wait for Terrence now."

"That's everything." The older woman placed her hand on top of Carrie's shivering hand. "You take good care of yourself, sweetie pie." Her warmth seemed to melt away Carrie's worries for a moment.

Carrie read the name engraved on the pin hanging from the receptionist's turquoise scrubs. "Thank you, Marge." She turned to travel through the hospital to locate Terrence.

***

Carrie took a deep breath to maintain her composure. She finally gave in and asked a passing nurse for help. "Excuse me, where can I find Terrence Coleman?"

The confused nurse squinted her eyes. "You'll have to forgive me. I don't know who that is."

Carrie was quite embarrassed. "Oh, I'm sorry. Could you tell me how to get to the emergency surgery waiting area?"

"Oh, sure, continue on your path and make a left when you reach the end of the hall. Just take the elevators up to the fifth floor. That's where the patients are taken with emergency procedures."

"Thank you. Sorry if I disturbed you." Carrie waved goodbye.

"No problem. Just ask one of the nurses at the station located by the waiting room for the patient's condition."

Carrie took a deep breath as she marched to her destination, where she finally found the nurses' station. "Excuse me, could someone help me?"

"Quickly please, I have patients to see," a nurse replied.

"Hello, I've been here since early this morning and I was told, Terrence Coleman, was out of surgery and would be moved to a room on this floor. Could you please tell me if he's been moved to his room yet?"

"What is your relationship to the patient ma'am?" The nurse rolled her eyes.

Carrie looked at the clock. "I'm his girlfriend. Please, I've been here since ten o'clock this morning. It's two o'clock. I need to know something."

"We can only give that type of information to the family," the thin nurse grabbed a red folder from the counter and walked away.

"Wait. Hold on. Hey, *excuse me*. Could someone please *help* me?" Carrie smacked the counter.

A nurse standing close-by motioned for Carrie to follow her to the other side of the waiting room. She whispered Terrence's updates from a small portable tablet. "The bullet was removed and the damaged organs were saved with no permanent injuries. He needed a few stitches. He'll remain in the operating room for just a while longer so they can monitor him as the anesthesia tapers off and then he'll be moved to room 503."

"Okay, well I see nothing has changed because the doctor told me the same thing. So, I guess that means he's still hanging in there. Thank you for being so considerate unlike your co-worker."

"I completely understand your concerns. He's your loved one. I'm sorry the other nurse was so short with you. Sometimes we do this for so long we lose our compassion. Terrence appears to be a really strong man. You have no need to worry. If you hang out here, I'll let you know when he will be moved to his room but keep in mind it may be a while before that happens."

Carrie yawned placing her long legs in the two empty seats beside her and closed her eyes to sleep for a while. She still felt drowsy from the medication the doctor gave her to help with the soreness from her horrible encounter with Ronald.

***

The nurse touched Carrie's leg, and whispered, "Ma'am, Mr. Coleman has been taken to his room if you'd like to see him."

"Thank you so much. Is he awake? Can he talk?" Carrie fired off all her questions.

"Yes, he can talk. However, he's still a little groggy from the anesthetic."

Carrie wandered down the hall until she reached room 503. She softly tapped the door and proceeded to walk in. "Hey, Terrence, how are you feeling?"

"I'm a little sore, but I'd rather know how you're feeling," he replied, moving his blanket away from his face.

"I'm okay. Did they tell you how long you will need to be here?"

"Yeah, I just need to stay overnight. As long as they can see everything still works, I can get out of here as early as tomorrow." Terrence smiled.

"I can't believe they would let you out so soon. I want you to come to my house until you're feeling better. I don't know if that's something you want to do but I'd like to repay you for all you've done for me. I don't know but something changed inside of me when you took that bullet. I just feel so protected by you and I love this feeling this way," Carrie replied caressing Terrence's chest.

Terrence smiled. "I think any real man would have done the same if he were in my shoes, but I can't stay in your home and invade your space like that."

"Trust me, you're not in the way. But, if you've made other plans, I totally understand," Carrie looked down at the tiled floor.

"I was thinking of staying with parents but they haven't heard about any of this and I'm actually reluctant to tell them."

"I get that you want to avoid them worrying about you but you should let your family know what happened. But, please say you'll stay with me. I need to be there for you the same way you were there for me."

"Okay, I'll stay with you," Terrence surrendered.

Carrie whispered in his ear, "I'm going home to take a long hot bath and get a little rest. I'll be back first thing in the morning." She kissed his cheek goodbye.

***

Carrie hurried out of the hospital and flagged the first cab to get home. She sat in the warm backseat and wondered what could have happened to her if Terrence wouldn't have shown up when he did. Carrie had many thoughts bouncing in her head on the ride home. "Oh, hey could you wait here for one second and I'll run inside to get your cash." she explained to the cab driver.

"Sure, take your time. The meter is still running lady," the driver replied.

Carrie stood, momentarily paralyzed by the thoughts of what had occurred. The blood from Ronald shooting Terrence was still on her marble floor in the foyer. She quickly grabbed her purse to pay the driver. "Thank you for waiting. Have a great day." She hurried back inside to take a hot shower but noticed the red light blinking on her answering machine. Carrie pushed the button and walked away but could still hear the computerized voice announcing each message,

You have three messages. Message one. "Hey, Carrie. Baby, it's me, Davion... I'm back."

Carrie stopped and stood still.

Message two, the answering machine continued to play. "*Carrie, give me a call at (555) 543-3396.*"

Message three. "*I'm staying at the Sheraton Hotel in room 185. Please come by later, we need to talk. Scratch that, I'll come by your place around five o'clock.* Davion spoke in a rushed voice."

Carrie glanced at the round silver clock hanging on the wall to see she had less than twenty minutes before Davion would arrive at the time he promised. Dashing through the house, she picked up things that had been knocked over. Carrie grabbed every cleaning supply she thought would clean the foyer. She scrubbed the entire area as best she could with limited time.

At five o'clock Davion rang the doorbell as planned.

"I see you're still punctual as ever," she stood in the door pushing her supplies to the side with her foot.

"Carrie baby, I missed you so much. I moved back baby. Aren't you happy to see me," Davion asked kissing her as he entered her house.

"What are you doing? I haven't laid eyes on you in over a year and here you are acting like we're still engaged." Carrie cried wiping the stream of tears from her eyes.

"Hey, no, don't cry, honey. I just wanted to let you know I've moved back to L.A. We have so much to catch up on." He gave her a passionate kiss as she wept.

Carrie snapped out of her trance, and broke free of his grasp. "How can you come in here and act like it's only been yesterday since you've been gone. It's been a year, Davion. A damn year without any contact!"

"Baby, I'm sorry. I wanted to call you, but I felt it would just make things worse. How are your parents doing?"

"If you really cared, you would have made the call yourself long before this conversation. You have every number to all of my family member's but it seems like you don't care to speak to anyone ever since you decided to more. You left me in every way possible Davion. How dare you stand here and act like what you did was okay." Carrie pounded her finger into Davion's chest.

"That's not true, Carrie. I wanted you to come with me, but you didn't want that. I thought you had given up on us. I wasn't sure if your family would be receptive of my calling. I didn't want to cause any unwanted drama," Davion explained holding her shaking hands.

"You knew I had obligations here. Why would you even ask me to walk away from my law firm? It's not just a job Davion. I started that firm. I work for myself. I couldn't leave everything I worked so hard to build to run behind you and you didn't even try after you left. Davion, it's been a year and I know you've been in other relationships. So, why are you here?" Carrie sat down in a nearby chair.

Davion knelt down in front of Carrie. "I won't lie to you. Yes, I've had other relationships, but they never lasted because I kept comparing every woman I dated to you. No one could ever fill your shoes, honey. You're who I'm destined to be with."

"That's just too bad for you Davion because my eyes are wide open and my heart is on probation. I will not be lead on pure emotions this time. The fact of the matter is you abandoned me and left me to pick up the pieces of my broken heart and you didn't even care to make one phone call to even check on me."

"Oh, I get it. You're seeing someone else." Davion stood taking a deep breath.

Carrie shook her head. "Yes, I am, Davion. I'm seeing someone else. You left that door wide open for another man to step up and do something you just couldn't seem to follow through with." Davion stroked Carrie's hair. She stood and walked toward the door. "No, don't play with my hair. Don't act like you're my man now that you know there is someone else in the picture."

"You know as well as I do I'm the only man for you. We complete each other." He said wrapping his arms around her waist.

"No, Davion, no touching, okay? I never thought in a million years you would come back into my life. I had no choice but to move on."

"I have a late meeting to attend, but I'll be calling you later tonight to talk some sense into your head."

Carrie placed her hand on the door. "Before you go, I have one more thing to tell you." She paused, closed her eyes, and with a slight hitch in her breath and said, "This morning I was raped—"

Davion interrupted. "*What*? No. Are you okay?"

"Allow me to finish what I'm saying, please. The man who almost raped me tried to shoot me, but Terrence took a bullet that was meant for me. I've asked him to stay with me until he's better."

"How long have you known this Terrence guy?" Davion asked.

"I don't have to answer that."

"I can tell by your reply it hasn't been long enough to move him in so quickly. I mean I am grateful myself he did what he did for you but damn Carrie. You don't have to move that man in here. Especially with you feeling so venerable."

"I didn't say he was moving in here. I'm simply showing my appreciation. He didn't have to do what he did. I will always be indebted to him for that."

"Thanking him for what he did for you is enough appreciation. Moving him in is simply out of order. I'll definitely be calling you tonight. You're trying to replace me, but you can't replace me. You just can't do that. I won't let it happen." Davion moved in closer and kissed her lips.

"Stop that Davion. I'll talk to you later. Please leave." Carrie held the door open.

"You've changed. I'm starting to feel like I don't know who you are."

"I'm the same woman I was when you left me. I've just moved on."

"Sweetheart, you were raped and you don't want me to be here for you. This is not the Carrie I know and love. Let me be here for you. I can't leave you knowing this is going on. I love you way too much. I could never do that to you."

"What about this late meeting you just told me you needed to attend?"

"I don't care about a meeting. I care about you," Davion replied with tears in his big brown eyes.

"No, please just go. I'll be fine." She pushed Davion out the door.

"Please don't do this, Carrie. Don't shut me out."

"I promise I'll talk to you soon. I've been through a lot today. I just want to get some sleep."

"Promise me one thing," Davion asked.

"What's that?"

"I want you to call me if you need anything. I don't care what time. Early in the morning or late at night. If you're afraid of being alone tonight or if you're hurting, please, just call and I'll be right over."

"I would do that but I don't want to end up right back where we were before you left me like nothing happened. I'll call you soon." She closed the door.

Chapter Five

Carrie was all smiles as she was getting herself together to go back to the hospital to pick up Terrence. He would be coming home with her. Wearing her red and gray plaid strapless dress accented with her red high heels, Carrie grabbed her red clutch, and headed out the door. She knew holding on to what happened to her could possibly destroy the strong woman she embodied. So she took a deep breath and spoke a prayer for strength as she walked out the door to her car. From that day forth she was walking by faith. All the Christian values her mother had given she and her sister kicked in full gear. She would need that in order for her to deal with the things Ronald had done to her and tried to take away from her.

This time she didn't drive with her windows down or music loud. She needed to think on her drive over. Davion's words pierced in her head. He knew her better than anyone knew her and she questioned her decision to bring Terrence into her home. Was she using Terrence to get over Davion or did she really feel this was the best way to thank him? When Carrie arrived at the hospital, she parked at the main entrance. She walked through the hospital with her large black shades on and waved at the staring people as she passed by. She tapped on the counter when she arrived at the nurse's station.

"Hello. How may I help you?" a pudgy nurse asked.

"Yes, I'm here to pick up Terrence Coleman. Is there anything I need to do?"

"No, ma'am, he's already signed his paperwork. He's been anxiously waiting to go."

"Thank you," Carrie replied smoothing her shiny, shoulder-length hair.

"Take care of him. Have a great day." The nurse waved goodbye.

Carrie slowly entered the small room when she noticed a petite woman sitting on the hospital bed next to Terrence. The mysterious woman had long, wavy, jet black hair pulled into a ponytail and the cutest set of dimples.

Terrence jumped when Carrie cleared her throat as she entered the room. "Oh, hey, what are you doing here so early?"

"Early, my butt. The nurse called and said you were ready to be discharged. It looks like you made other plans." Carrie flung her arms as she spoke.

"This is my sister, Rolonda Coleman." Terrence smirked.

"Oh, I feel so silly. It's really nice to meet you. I thought you were some random woman here with him." Carrie pushed her hair behind her ears.

"Oh that's okay. I'm a woman so I know how you feel. It's nice to actually meet you. Terrence has been talking about you all morning. He said you were a cutie, but he failed to mention just how beautiful you really are." Rolonda embraced Carrie.

"Thank you, I wished he would've told me you would be here this morning. Then I could've avoided embarrassing myself. Terrence never told me he had a sister. How old are you, if you don't mind me asking?"

"Oh, I don't mind. I'm twenty-eight years old as of yesterday. So, you could imagine how upsetting it was to hear that my big brother was in the hospital."

Carrie jumped from the sound of something moving behind her. "I'm sorry, I didn't know there was someone else in the room. How are you doing?" Carrie reached out to greet the older woman seated by the far window.

"I'm blessed, honey. My name is Edith Coleman. I'm Terrence's mother."

"Nice to meet you, Mrs. Coleman." Carrie shook the older woman's wrinkled hand.

"I'm pleased to meet you. Terrence has been going on and on about you all morning, baby," she said searching through her purse.

Carrie smiled. "Oh, he has. I hope it's been good things."

The nurse barged in the room handing Carrie a stack of papers. "Sorry for interrupting. Mr. Coleman, I have all of your paperwork in order and you're all set to go."

"Oh, honey, are you sure you don't want your old Mom to take care of you?" Edith asked.

"If you would prefer to go home with your mom it's totally okay with me. I just thought if you came home with me it would be a nice way for me to show you my appreciation," Carrie interjected.

"No, I'm going home with you as planned. Mom, please stop fussing over me. Rolonda I can always tell when you are hiding something. Stop worrying about me. Your big brother is fine."

"I can't help but worry about you. Are you sure this guy isn't going to show up at your house again Carrie? I don't know if I could handle anything else happening to my brother."

"I'm sure he won't be coming back. He's in jail and besides I'm getting bars put up on the windows this week," Carrie assured Rolonda.

"Well, I think you both are being a bit careless. Son, you were shot and you want to go back where it happened." Edith shook her head.

"I spoke with the detective and Ronald is still in jail. My neighbor has called a company to come out and have bars placed on all the windows and doors. No one is ever going to break into my home again," Carrie replied.

"I hear what you're saying, but as a mother I can't help worry. Terrence is my only son. It causes me so much stress and pain to see my kids hurt."

"I understand Mrs. Coleman. Again, I'm not forcing Terrence to stay with me. I'd be okay if he wants to stay with you. It will not hurt my feelings in the slightest way." Carrie placed her hand over her chest.

"Mom, Rolonda, I love you guys. But, I'm going home with Carrie. Here's the address. I'm sure she won't mind if you guys came over to check on me." He scribbled Carrie's address on a piece of paper.

"No, I don't mind at all. In fact, I insisted you come over. I think it'll give everyone some peace."

"I don't know about peace, but thank you honey. It was nice to meet you. I hope I didn't hurt your feelings but this is my baby and I worry about him. Son, call me as soon as you get in. I love you." Mrs. Coleman gathered her things.

"I love you more. Get over here Rolonda. Stop worrying I'll be fine." He hugged his sister.

"You better take care of yourself. I love you," Rolonda replied.

The nurse returned. "I have your wheels. Are you ready to go," she asked.

"I don't need a wheelchair."

"Now Mr. Coleman, didn't you tell me you were on the executive board of another hospital?" the nurse asked.

"Yes, I am."

"Well, you know this is hospital policy. Now, let me help you into the chair." The nurse stood beside Terrence with her hands out.

Terrence struggled to move to the edge of the bed. "Rules are rules."

***

Carrie eased her car into the garage and hurried to help Terrence out of the car. "I have the guest room ready for you."

"Wait, I thought I would be staying in the same room with you," Terrence asked.

Carrie gasped. "We agreed to take things slow, right?"

"I don't want to have sex with you, Carrie. I want to be close to you in case I need your help in the middle of the night. I promise I'll stay on my side of the bed and I never break a promise." Terrence held his two fingers up Boy Scout style.

Carrie nodded continuing down the hall to her bedroom. "Oh, I'm sorry for jumping to conclusions. I'm still a little on edge with all of this. Well, I guess you could sleep with me. All I ask is that you respect my wishes and don't try anything. I'm not open to sex with anyone especially after what's happened."

"No need to worry. I'm not that type of guy and besides I am not in the mood for sex with a bullet would and surgical pains. I would never pressure you with sex knowing what Ronald has done to you."

"Thank you for understanding." She smiled.

"I don't mean to cut the conversation short but my medicine has me pretty sleepy right now," Terrence said stretching out on the bed.

"Okay, you get some sleep. Don't forget you told your mom you would call her later."

"She'll be okay. I'll call her in the morning." Terrence yawned.

"I don't really believe that but get some sleep." Carrie closed the blinds and drew the curtains. She tip toed to her armoire to retrieve her night clothes to join Terrence in some much needed sleep. It was still early but after everything the two had gone through, sleep was a must.

***

Carrie typed away on her computer at work that morning. She sipped another cup of coffee as she completed her notes for her clients before ending her day until she was interrupted by soft taps on her office door.

"Hi Carrie. Do you have a minute to talk?" Debra eased in the office.

"Of course, please, come in."

"We have all been so worried about you. How are you feeling?"

"First, thank you guys for caring and thank you for the beautiful flowers. I'm doing much better. Thank God I asked Terrence to come over early that morning."

"Yes, that was a blessing. I just wanted to check on you and see what state of mind you were in. I don't want to bother you too much. Is there anything else you need me to do before I head out for the day," Debra asked.

"No, you have done more than enough. We are so fortunate to have you here. You enjoy the rest of your evening."

"Okay, I'm going to grab those files you needed and reroute the phones. You have a good night."

Carrie saved her notes and powered down her computer. She grabbed her briefcase, turned off the lights, and locked the door to her office. "Hey Kathy, where have you been all day?" She stood in the hallway.

"I've been out trying to get some things done for this case I'm working on. I didn't think you would be back to work so soon. I just stopped to grab some documents I need for this case I'm working on. How are you? Come on, I'll walk you to your car." Kathy repositioned the stack of files in her arms.

"I'm as good as can be expected." Carrie replied.

Kathy continued her pace to the parking lot with Carrie. "What's going on with Ronald?"

"He's still in jail for now." Carrie switched the heavy briefcase to her other hand to grab her keys.

"Do you think he will get out anytime soon?"

"I don't know. He's having a preliminary hearing to try and get bail. I don't think I could handle it if he were to get out." Carrie disarmed her alarm on her car to place her briefcase and purse inside.

"I think I should go in your place. I don't think you should see him right now."

"Oh my God, that would be great. You would do that for me?" Carrie asked smiling.

"Yes, I would. I'm your partner for God's sake. I'll make some calls and get the details. You need to take some time off. I know you said work helps you forget about things but maybe, rather than trying to forget about it, you should try talking to someone. I have everything under control here." Kathy walked toward her car.

"Wait a minute Kathy. You're good but even you can't handle the case load we have alone. I couldn't leave everything on you like that. Besides, I've never been the type of person who can sit around with nothing to do."

"Well, at least go to a psychologist to talk about it. I've got to run. Love you much." She blew kisses in the air to Carrie.

"Love you more." Carrie sat in her car to head home. She drove across town wondering how Terrence managed to get around the house by himself all day. For the first time since she had her house built she thought about the size possibly being a bit too much.

Terrence heard the garage door opening. He limped toward the door to greet Carrie. "Hey there. How was your day?" He led her to the dining room.

"It was really long and boring. I thought about you most of the day." She noticed candles flickering as she neared the dining room.

"You make me feel so special. Oh, and you have a message. He said his name was Davion." Terrence read the note he jotted down. "He said he wants you to meet him at the Cappuccino/Espresso Café at eight-thirty tonight. I figured it was important." He handed her the small piece of paper.

"Wow, this is really important. Would you be okay if I go to that later?" She held the paper up.

Terrence shrugged and grabbed her hand. "No, I don't mind. I cooked for you."

Carrie felt somewhat crappy for not explaining to Terrence who Davion was to her but all those thoughts went away when she walked into the candle lit dining room. "You didn't have to do this for me. You've lit candles and everything. You shouldn't be up doing all this when you're trying to recover."

"I wanted to do something special for you because you've been so nice to me. Why are you crying?" Terrence asked, wiping her tears away.

"I'm happy. This was very nice of you. I really appreciate this."

"Don't get all teary-eyed on me. Do you like the music?" Terrence poured red wine into long-stemmed glasses.

"Yes, I love it and I appreciate you doing all this for me. It's been a really long time since I've had someone do this for me."

"Oh, I don't mind at all. I actually miss doing things like this for someone. You really have a beautiful home. It kind of makes me feel like I didn't put much effort into the décor of my condo," Terrence laughed.

"The décor. Now that's a word you don't hear a man say too often."

"Ouch, that hurt. Are you saying my manhood is questionable using words like décor?" Terrence took a bite of his food.

"No, no, I wouldn't go that far," Carrie laughed sipping her wine.

"Good, because I can be more macho if that's what you like."

"No, don't change anything about yourself. I happen to like you just the way you are."

"That's what I like to hear. Most women try to change everything about a man into what she thinks he should be when they begin any type of relationship."

"I'm not that kind of woman. If I don't like who you are then I simply won't give you the time of day."

"Dang, you're the real deal Miss Lady." Terrence took a big bite of his food.

Carrie laughed. "Wow, this tastes as good as the food at your restaurant."

"You don't grow up with a chef and not learn a thing or two."

"I'll have to give you brownie points for this. There's nothing more sexy than a man who knows is way around a kitchen."

Terrence smiled. "That's good because I want you to feel like you found a winner in me."

After the two finished eating, Carrie changed into a pair of denim jeans with a yellow cotton halter top, and her new multi-colored Pastry athletic shoes. "I'll be back, I'm going to that meeting. Hopefully this won't take too long. Thank you again for cooking. Everything was really great."

"No problem at all. You take your time and do what you need to do."

"Thank you for understanding," Carrie replied, fleeing from the house. She tapped her fingers on the steering wheel on her drive to the Café. *"I don't know what you are trying to accomplish Davion, but you picked a fine time to come back into my life,"* she mumbled to herself. Carrie arrived at the Café but sat in her car for a moment to get her thoughts together. She took a deep breath and stepped out the car to make the treacherous walk into the crowded Café.

Davion stood to show Carrie to her seat. "Hello, beautiful. I see this guy actually gives you your messages."

"Trust me. I had mixed feelings about meeting you tonight."

"Why would you even feel the need to think twice about seeing me?"

"Because I know what you want." Carrie fiddled with her car keys.

"Okay, then tell me why I asked you to come here tonight." Davion powered off his ringing cell phone.

"You want me to put Terrence out and jump back into a relationship with you."

"If that's what you think I want, then what would be your thoughts about that?" Davion asked.

"You know I've never been a fan of the 'what if games'. Just get to the point and cut the small talk."

Davion responded, pushing a long envelope in front of Carrie. "I have two tickets in this envelope to the Caribbean and I want you to go with me in two weeks."

Carrie smiled. "That's impossible. I don't think I will have to time for that right now Davion."

"Find the time for me, baby. I really need time alone with you for a couple days. We have a lot of stuff we need to talk about. You know I'm not going away that easily when I feel the way I do about you baby."

"I can't give you an answer right now. Give me a couple days."

"Baby, take all the time you need. I'm just happy you're thinking about it."

"Is that all you wanted?"

Davion brushed Carrie's hair away from her face with his hand. "No, you know I want to know about this guy you're shacking up with. What do you know about him?"

"Don't go there Davion." Carrie gazed out the large window.

"Don't be that way, baby. You're a very successful woman and there are a lot of men who will try to prey on you just because of your success. I want to make sure you're thinking clearly. I was wrong for leaving and I don't want you to do this because of what I did to you."

"Don't worry about me. Let me make my own decisions. I'm a big girl. I'll call you in a few days about the trip," she said.

Davion stared into Carrie's eyes. "I love you, Carebear. Please, don't treat me like this for caring about your well-being."

"I love you, too but you leaving me helped me to become stronger and a bit selfish to do the things that make me happy." Carrie stood only to disappear in dark night to once again journey across town to be with Terrence.

***

Terrence was becoming stronger as the weeks passed. It was finally time him to go back home. "I just wanted to thank you again for allowing me to be here with you. I'm going to miss you while you're out of town. But, I know business is business so I understand."

Carrie placed her bulky luggage by the front door and said, "You're looking really good, Terrence. You got better quicker than I thought you would."

"Well, I guess that's why they call me superman. Now, let's get you to the airport, and I need you to do me a big favor.

"Sure, anything," Carrie replied.

"If it's not asking too much of you. Could you call me every day your away?"

"I'll do the best I can if I'm not too busy. Are you ready to go? I have a plane to catch," Carrie avoided making promises she didn't intend to keep.

"Excuse me Diva but your phone is ringing," Terrence laughed.

"Let the machine get it." Carrie strolled to the car.

"I guess you want me to get your luggage," Terrence laughed, listening to the recording message.

***

Carrie tugged on her blue bikini as she stood alone to make a much needed call. "It's so nice to hear your voice," she whispered.

"What do you want?" Terrence replied.

"I thought you wanted me to call you as often as I could, or did you forget about that request?"

"Have you been busy at work?" Terrence asked.

"I'll be a much more happy camper when I'm home and I can see you again."

"Why don't you tell me the truth," Terrence huffed.

"I don't understand this attitude you have with me right now."

"I'm not a fool, Carrie. I heard the message on your answering machine the day I took you to the airport. Davion called to tell you he was running late, but he would be there before take-off. You two went to the Caribbean together but you failed to tell me the truth. It's not like we talked about being that exclusive."

Carrie placed her face into her hand. "I didn't tell you because I didn't think you would understand. I had to go with Davion because I had to see if we still had anything between us."

"You could've found out about that at the Café. Yes, I remembered his name and I recognized his voice on the answering machine."

"I would apologize to you but honestly I don't owe you an explanation. Just like you said a moment ago. We're not serious. Selfishly I'm doing what I need to do for me," Carrie replied.

"I hope you find what you're looking for." Terrence ended the call.

***

Carrie was finally home after her trip with Davion and her machine was full of messages. She decided not to listen but make one call to someone who she felt would be waiting and willing to hear from her with no drama.

"Hello?" Janitta answered out of breath.

"Hey J, how are you doing?"

"Where the hell have you been? I've been calling you like crazy!" Janitta screamed into the phone.

"Oh, I forgot to tell you. I went to the Caribbean with Davion."

Janitta squealed, "Oh, my God. What's up with that? Are you guys picking up where you left off?"

"Yeah right. We just needed time alone away from everyone to talk about things. He's going to give me time to see what I want."

"That sounds like a plan to me. What happened with Ronald's stupid behind?"

"I have no idea yet. I have to check on that tomorrow. He really did lose his stupid mind."

"I totally second that. I can't believe he would be so stupid. All I could think was the worst when I didn't hear from you. Hell, I've called the police station and hospitals looking for your butt. I even drove by your house to go inside and make sure you weren't tied to a chair or something. I can't believe you took off after the stuff that went down and not think to call me."

"Oh my goodness you're like a mother hen J. You need to have some babies because it sounds like it's about that time."

Janitta laughed, "Whatever, you just need to learn how to pick up a phone selfish lady. So, what happened to your other tenderroni?"

Carrie took a deep breath. "I haven't talked to Terrence. I kind of lied to him and told him I was going out of town on business. But little did I know he heard a message on my answering machine from Davion the day we were leaving. I went to the car ahead of him so I didn't know Davion had called. He was spilling his guts about us going to the Caribbean. Girl, when he called me out on my lie I was mortified."

Janitta gasped. "Cold busted your behind. But, serves you right. You knew you didn't have to go away with Davion if you claim you don't want to be with him anymore. I think you're lying to all of us and yourself about Davion. You know you love that man's dirty drawers."

Carrie laughed, "Janitta, you're a woman. You of all people know how hard it is to make your heart do what your mind tells it to do. I needed that trip with Davion. We have a lot of issues to work out."

"If you don't want the man anymore there are no issues to work out. I'm not Terrence, you can't lie to me honey. How did Terrence handle the truth when he busted you?"

"Heck, he hung up in my face." Carrie played with her curly locks.

"Oh, that's harsh. Yeah, he's pretty pissed. What are you going to do?" Janitta asked.

"I'm not going to do anything about it. I can't make that man understand my point of view. I have other things to focus on other than worrying about Terrence."

"Yes; Ronald being the main thing you need to focus on. What are the police prepared to do with him?" Janitta asked.

"I'm going to the police department in the morning to find out. I really don't want to ease up on this. I shouldn't have gone away right now. I should've stayed here to put a little pressure on the D.A. with this case."

"Well, I didn't want to say anything but you're right. You should've had your butt at home taking care of business. But no, you want to cat around with Davion," Janitta laughed.

"Really Janitta. I was catting around? Davion wished he had this cat. He didn't even get to sniff around it for your information."

"Yeah right. You could never say no to that man. Next week, you'll be telling me a different story. You guys will be back together like nothing ever happened."

"Trust me Miss Know It All. You won't get that call."

"Okay all jokes aside, I'll be praying for you with the Ronald stuff. You should really think about talking to someone about what happened to you. I love you like a play cousin but I need to get going."

Carrie laughed. "I love you, too J. I'll talk to you later. I need to take a long hot bath."

"Yeah, go wash that sin away," Janitta laughed.

"You're on a roll tonight," Carrie replied saying her goodbyes to Janitta. That night she tossed and turned until the sunlight shined through her blinds. She laid there staring at the ceiling wondering what news the D.A. would have for her about Ronald. She finally mustered up the courage to get out of bed to get herself dressed and out the door. Before leaving, she stood at her desk getting her file together to state her case to the D.A and ensure everyone would be on the same page. She once again said a silent prayer.

***

Carrie crawled to other side of her bed to answer her ringing phone. "Hello," she answered.

"How are you?" the caller asked.

"Who is this?"

"Terrence. Have you already forgotten about me?"

"Oh, I'm kind of in a funky mood. I just left the D.A.'s office only to find out Ronald was released on bail and he never showed up to court. Now these geniuses can't find him," Carrie replied.

"That's bullshit. After all that man did they shouldn't have ever let him out. Damn, I hate to hear that. How have you been?"

"I'm doing well. I can't complain."

"Good, because I wanted to ask if you've made a decision about who you want to be with?" He asked.

"There was no decision to be made. I told you we basically said our goodbyes and closed the door to that chapter."

"Okay, I hear what you're saying about Davion but what do you want to do about us?" Terrence inquired.

"I thought we were trying to be more than friends but you haven't listened to anything I had to say."

"You would've reacted the same way I did if the shoe was on the other foot. You handled the situation really shitty Carrie."

"You're right. I would've been one mad chick. But dang Terrence, you hung up on me and I haven't heard from you since then. Now you want to know about us but you haven't acted like there was an us."

"I'd like to make up for shutting you out. Why don't you come over to my place tonight," Terrence asked.

"I don't think I have anything planned. What time should I come over?" Carrie asked.

"I'm on your time sweetie."

"How about seven o'clock?" Carrie implied.

"Like I said. It's all on you. I'll be here when you decide to come over."

Carrie smiled and immediately ran into her walk-in closet to search for her killer outfit for the night. She lucked up on a dress she'd been saving for a special night out. Carrie closed her eyes to enjoy her shower before heading to Terrence's house. She took one last look at her flawless reflection and adjusted her navy strapless dress she'd accented with her silver jewelry. Carrie headed out to her car to reconnect with her beau.

***

Terrence stood outside to greet Carrie when she arrived. "Aren't you the eager beaver." Carrie parked and stepped out to greet her antsy date.

"I'm excited to see you. Wow, You look great."
Terrence gawked.

"Thank you," she smiled.

"I'm really happy you came over tonight," he said
opening the door to his condo.

"Wow, this is nice." She smiled at the glowing candles.

"I thought it would be a nice peace offering." Terrence
caressed her hand.

"I could get used to this. Maybe we'll have to fight
more often than I'd like if you go these lengths to make
up." Carrie allowed Terrence to escort her to his dining
table.

Terrence placed several small kisses on the nape of her
neck and shoulders. Carrie could feel his warm, moist
breath with each kiss. "I want to please you in every way,"
he whispered.

Carrie's chest filled with air. She took heavy breaths
and arched her back. Her body filled with passion. "Um,
that feels great." She turned her chair to face Terrence.

Terrence bent over to give Carrie a soft kiss on her
trembling lips. "You smell sweet. I wonder how you taste."

Carrie uttered, "Why don't you find out?"

Terrence reached up her short dress to remove her silk
unmentionables. "I like these." He tossed her panties over
his shoulder to the floor. He spread her legs and buried his
face to devour her in whole.

"Oh," she cried out.

Terrence helped Carrie to her feet. He stood behind her
and unzipped her dress where it fell to the tan carpeted
floor. She turned and gazed into his eyes and removed her
gold-corseted bra. He cupped her full breasts and lightly
brushed her tiny nipple with his salivating tongue.

"Follow me." Terrence led her to another room.

Carrie followed his lead to an awaiting bathtub filled
with bubbles and red rose petals. "Wow, this was
presumptuous of you."

"I told you I want to please you in every way possible." He sat behind Carrie in the warm water and positioned her to sit on top of his rigid manhood. She took the lead and rocked her body back and forth to please her lover. Carrie rested her head on Terrence's shoulder. He moved her frizzing hair to the side and wrapped his arms around her petite waist and held her tightly to match each bounce. Terrence rubbed her secreting clitoris with his large fingers. "Damn, you feel so good," he cried out.

Carrie moaned. "Please Terrence, don't stop. I'm almost there."

He nibbled her neck and held her in his arms until he could join her in climax. "How do you feel?"

"Complete," Carrie replied relaxing in Terrence's arms.

"Good, I want to keep you satisfied." The couple retreated from the tub and dried off. He led Carrie to his large bed for the night where they slept in each other's arms.

***

The chirping birds alerted the lovers of the new day. Terrence intertwined his fingers with Carrie's while they lounged in the cozy bed to watch the sunrise. "Why did you really decide to go away with your ex?" he asked.

Carrie turned to face Terrence as she spoke, "I wanted to know if I was really over Davion. You have to understand. We were together for a very long time. When I went on the first date with you it was something about you that reminded me so much of Davion. You two are very different, but you both romance me the same way. The one thing that still stung in my heart was knowing how much time had passed since I was with Davion. We still have major issues between us."

"For future references, I can pretty much handle anything you throw my way. Trust me on that."

Carrie smiled. "I guess I underestimated you."

"You guess you underestimated me?" Terrence repeated.

"Okay, fine. I was wrong." They laughed.

"You're so beautiful in the morning."

"You make me feel like a schoolgirl. But, this school girl better get home. I can't be all out for days at a time like this. I'm way too grown for this. Besides, I don't even know where we're going with this. I knew last night I was moving too fast but I just couldn't help myself," Carrie said.

"You pretty much know where I want this to go. There's no way I would've called you back if I didn't want to at least try to see where we could take this. But, do you really need to go right now. We just got into this morning glow thing."

"Yes, I really need to go. I had a great time with you handsome. I know I've been a bit inaccessible since the whole Ronald ordeal, but you have been so patient and I really appreciate it."

"Trust me baby, you were worth the wait."

Carrie walked away to retrieve her dress. "By the way, I see you had some great moves last night."

"Well, you know I do what I can." He proudly stuck his chest out and walked to kiss his mate.

"No you're not prancing around like you're a big shot. You're something amazing. I'll call you later," she said.

Chapter Six

Carrie sat on the sofa and gasped at what she saw. She managed to complete her call even with her quivering hands.

"Hello?" Terrence answered.

"Do you have a moment. We really need to talk," Carrie said.

"I've always got time for you sweetheart."

"I don't quite know how to say this, so I'm just going to say it. I'm late."

"Late for what?" Terrence asked.

"What do you think? My cycle, my time of the month. Use your head baby."

"Are you serious? It's only been four months. This can't happen right now. I mean, we always use protection."

"I know that and I'm just as surprised as you about all this."

"Okay, calm down. I'll buy a pregnancy test and come right over," Terrence replied.

"I've already taken four tests and congratulations. You're going to be a daddy," Carrie sang.

"Wow, this is happening fast. Have you made a doctor's appointment?"

"No, I just found out I was pregnant like two seconds ago. Just get over here as soon as you can. We need to sit down and get a game plan. Oh, and before you bring it up. I don't do abortions. That's out of the question."

"I would never tell you what to do with your body. I'm a grown man and I made the decision to play around so now I just have to man up and do what's right. I'll be there shortly, I'm on my way."

"Okay baby, I'll be waiting." Carrie sighed.

***

Terrence banged on the door. "Come in, it's unlocked.

"How are you feeling," he asked.

"I'm fine. Sit down."

Terrence shook his head. "I have something I need to say. I've been through this whole baby thing with my ex-girlfriend, Cynthia. I was excited to become a dad. I went out and bought everything the baby needed. But, when she had the baby, I found out it wasn't mine. The worst part of it all was the baby didn't make it. I couldn't forgive her but I also couldn't leave her all alone to deal with the loss of her first born. What I'm trying to say is I want a DNA test. It's not that I don't trust you. It's for my peace of mind. I want to be able to fully enjoy this experience with you and not have anything in the back of my mind."

"I'm trying to wrap my head around what that has to do with me."

"If you're carrying my child, you have everything to do with how I'm feeling. I need you to put yourself in my position and do this for me."

"Does this have something to do with me going away with Davion. I told you we didn't have sex."

"I never thought about that. I explained to you why I'm asking you to do this. Is there a reason why you decided to bring that up right now?" Terrence asked.

"I feel like you're still holding that over my head. But, if this is something you need to do in order to be there for this child then I'll do whatever it takes. Because you're going to be in this child's life. I did not lay down by myself and make this child so I refuse to raise it alone."

"I want you to do this but I don't want you to hold it over my head later down the line."

"Whatever, I'll schedule the appointment and find out what our options are at this point." Carrie grabbed the phone and walked into the other room.

***

Carrie and Terrence approached a tall slender nurse behind the desk holding a clip board.

"Hi, may I help you?" the nurse asked.

"Yes, we are here for an appointment," Terrence replied.

"Okay, what are your names so we can get you all checked in." She sat down to type into the computer.

"I apologize, I'm a bit nervous. The appointment is under Carrie Johnson's. We have a paternity test scheduled," Carrie said.

"Oh, here it is. You're scheduled for the chronic villus sample today. So, congratulations on meeting your twelfth week. If you both could follow me, I'll explain the procedure a bit more and we can get you ready."

"Thank you," Carrie replied.

The nurse gathered the needed items and led Terrence and Carrie down a long hallway to an empty examination room. "Here we are. Please, have a seat. I would like to explain what we'll be doing today. You've made it to a safe time in your pregnancy for us to perform this test. We'll do this by inserting a thin flexible tube similar to this catheter." The nurse held up thin yellow tube. "The tube will be inserted through your vagina to your cervix until we reach the placenta to sample the baby's blood. Then we'll take blood samples from the both of you. Do you have any questions?"

"Could this be harmful to my baby if I do this?" Carrie asked.

"No, it's not harmful to the baby. It may cause cramping, leakage of your amniotic fluid, and vaginal spotting. But, these things are usually minor. It should all taper off and end within a day or two."

"How long will it take to get the results back?" Terrence asked.

The nurse glanced at Carrie's electronic chart. "The chromosome analysis usually takes up to four weeks. However, it appears the doctor has requested stat results. You should receive them within two weeks."

"Well, let's get this show on the road," Carrie mumbled.

"Before we get started, I need both of you to sign your paperwork. Your signatures will allow us to do this procedure. Ms. Johnson, you can change here and I'll return in just a moment." She handed Carrie a blue hospital gown and closed the door behind her.

"Why are you shaking?" Terrence asked.

"I'm a little nervous. This is all new to me and I'm praying this doesn't hurt the baby."

"I doubt the doctor would allow you to do this if there was a possibility it could hurt the baby."

There was a knock on the door and entered the room. "Hello Mrs. Johnson. It's nice to see you again."

"Oh, you know the doctor?" Terrence asked.

"Yes, he's been my OB/GYN for many years. Hi Doc. I see you finally made it back from your vacation," Carrie said smiling at him.

"Yes, it was a much needed get away. How have you been you feeling?" he asked.

"I feel great. I really haven't experienced much morning sickness so far."

"That's good with you being in your twelfth week. I'm happy to hear things are moving in a more positive direction after all that happened. Okay, so we're doing the chromosome analysis today."

"Yes we are."

"I need you to lie back and place your feet into each of the stirrups and relax your legs for me. I apologize in advance but you're going to feel a little discomfort when I put the tube in place."

"It's okay honey. I'm here," Terrence tried to comfort her.

The doctor gathered his last needed specimens. "I think we're all set. I'll allow you a moment to get dressed." The doctor and nurse vanished from the small examining room.

"I'm in a little pain. A bit more than he said it would be." Carrie held her stomach.

"I'll get the doctor back in here for you." Terrence reached for the door.

"No, don't do that. Just take me home so I can lie down. Maybe I can sleep the pain off for a while."

"Okay, take your time." He helped her off the tall examination table.

"Thank you for being here even though you just put me through agonizing pain because of your issues." Carrie dressed in her clothes.

"I thought you said you wouldn't hold this against me."

"I'm not okay but I'm in pain right now. So, I think I have a right to speak my mind," she said pouting.

"For what it's worth. Thank you for doing this."

"Yup, but you're going to feel pretty foolish when the results come back."

"I would rather feel foolish as the father than foolish thinking if I'm the dad or not later." The couple approached the receptionist area where the nurse was standing.

"Is there anything else we need to do?" Carrie asked.

"No, you're all set. We'll be in touch." The nurse waved goodbye.

"You guys have a nice day. Thank you again. Do you feel things are still moving too fast for you?"

"We did our best to prevent this from happening but that's life. You have to roll with the punches. Everything doesn't always go as planned. Maybe this happened for a reason. I mean, did you ever think you would've slowed down long enough to start a family without it just happening so suddenly?" Terrence held the door to open to help Carrie in the truck.

"I honestly couldn't say for sure if I would have slowed down to start a family. Maybe you're right."

"Well there you go. We both need to accept what's happening and embrace it. Come on, I'll get you in bed but I will be back later. I need to go back to the office for a while. I have a lot of work to do.

***

Terrence unlocked the door calling out to Carrie as he entered the house. "Good morning sleepy head."

"Why are you here so early?" Carrie sat on the edge of the bed rubbing her sleepy eyes.

"It's not early. It's ten o'clock. Today's the big day." Terrence sat two steaming hot cups of coffee on the chest of drawers near the door to her bedroom.

"Thanks for the coffee but I need to take a shower first baby."

"Sure, just remember we're running late."

"Terrence, really. Are you serious? You need to cool it and calm down. I'm not in the mood for anyone rushing me when I feel like I need to throw up everything I've ever eaten in life. My nerves are totally shot with you hounding around about this dang test."

A ringing phone interrupted their conversation. Carrie walked into the bathroom and ignored the ringing as Terrence stopped to answer. "Carrie Johnson's residence."

"Hello, this is Amy with the clinic, is Ms. Johnson available?"

"She's indisposed at this time. This is Terrence Coleman. You could speak with me."

"Oh yes, of course. We just wanted to confirm if you both would be coming to the office today for the results of your recent test," Amy questioned.

"Yes, we'll be there in about an hour."

"Great, I'll let the doctor know," She ended the call.

Terrence walked over to the bathroom door. "That was the clinic. They wanted to confirm we would be there today."

"Okay, I'm moving as fast as I can."

"No problem. Take your time I told her it would be about an hour."

"Good deal, thank you for that. This is not a pretty sight in here. For the last couple of days I've started to feel nauseated."

"Is there anything I can do or help make it better?" he asked.

Carrie replied walking out the bathroom. "Come on Terrence and let's get this over with so we can put all your doubts to rest."

"I couldn't agree with you more." The two walked downstairs into the garage.

Carrie replied entering the truck and buckling her seatbelt. "I'm sure you would agree. Since this was your idea."

"I can see now for sure you'll never live this down but I promise you I won't let you down." Terrence backed out the garage and slowly drove through the quiet neighborhood.

"I know you'll be a good father to our child but the fact that you needed this test in order to move forward raises a red flag about your trust issues." Carrie said taking in the scenery.

"It's not that I have trust issues with women. It's just a bad experience and I know that once I get the results this will renew my faith. I want to enjoy this experience with you." Terrence replied parking at the clinic.

"If that's how you feel, why have you been so distant this past week?" Carrie asked.

"Was I that obvious?"

"Yes, you were. What's going on?"

"Believe me when I say this has nothing to do with you. This DNA stuff has been heavy on my mind. It takes me back to a time in my life where I first experienced true pain. I really care for you and it would really hurt me if I wasn't the father of this child. I've been ready to become a father for a really long time. I just don't want it to be taken away from me for the second time. I don't know how I'd deal with that."

"I get that you feel a certain way about pregnancies. You don't have anything to worry about with me. Now, let's walk in here and leave all this behind us from this day on," Carrie said stepping out of the warm truck.

Terrence jogged to the passenger side to help Carrie out as always. "I trust you. I'm not worried anymore."

"Oh, well we can just go home then," Carrie laughed.

"No no, since we're here. Let's see what they have to say. We wouldn't want to waste their time and efforts."

"Yeah, sure. We wouldn't want to do that."

Carrie walked arm in arm with Terrence toward the receptionist desk.

"Hi Ms. Johnson. I see pregnancy looks good on you. Amy's ready for you. Go on back." The receptionist pushed a button to unlock the door.

"Thank you Alishia," Carrie replied walking through the door to meet her fate.

Amy dropped her pen. "How are you two doing this morning?"

"One of us is on edge," Carrie replied poking Terrence with her elbow.

"That's to be expected. It's totally normal in these situations," she replied.

"I could imagine." Carrie followed closely behind the nurse to an empty room.

"Now that we are in a secluded space I find joy in telling Mr. Coleman, congratulations, You're the father 99.9%."

Terrence had no words. He just beamed with pride.

***

As each month passed Carrie become less active at work. She stretched out on the sofa and played with her baby belly.

"Hello," she said answering the phone.

"Hey, Carrie, long time, no speak," Janitta said.

"I'm sorry. Don't be upset with me. Things have been very hectic."

"What's going on? It's not like you to not speak to me for months at a time. I didn't call you because I thought maybe you needed the space. I thought you were going through issues with the rape in all," Janitta rambled.

"I'm kind of embarrassed to say this because I know you're about to flip out on me. But, I'm pregnant J," Carrie replied.

"I know I did not just hear my best friend say she was pregnant."

"Yes, I'm pregnant."

"I can't understand how it slipped your mind to tell me about a baby. How far along are you?" she asked.

"I'm three months today."

"I'm going to let this go because I love you but who's the father?"

"Come on, Janitta, what kind of question is that?" Carrie asked.

"Well, you know you had that slip up with Davion. This baby is going to be a little cutie pie."

"I hope you're not going to hold this against me. You know I love you. I've just had so many changes and it all happened so fast. You're my girl and I love you."

"How could I be mad at my best friend, and besides, I have some news for you as well: William finally proposed," she squealed.

"After five long years he finally popped the question."

"Damn, what a way to bust my bubble, Carrie."

"I'm sorry. I just think he should've done this years before all the hurt, pain, and tears."

"It's better late than never then it all would have been in vain. We haven't officially set the date, but I was thinking somewhere around Valentine's Day."

"Send me an invitation. God willing, I'll be there," Carrie replied rubbing her belly.

"You better be. You're my Maid of Honor," Janitta replied.

"I love you and I trust you've thought about this from every angle. Oh hey J, Terrence is here. Could I call you later."

"Sure, bye mama-to-be." Janitta ended the call.

Carrie yelled sitting up on the sofa to hang up the cordless phone. "Use your key. Why do you always ring the doorbell like you don't have a key?"

Terrence walked in rambling away. "I always forget I have the dang thing."

"What are you doing here? I thought you wouldn't be in until later this evening?" Carrie asked.

"I wrapped work up early today. There's something important I need to ask you." Terrence said sitting beside Carrie on the sofa.

"Well, what could be so important you felt the need to take off work?"

Terrence slide from the sofa to knell on one knee. "I want you to see how much I love you. You're a special woman and you deserve nothing but the best. I appreciate you having my child and I would appreciate it even more if you would be my wife." He held a small blue box containing a 14-karat platinum diamond ring.

"Terrence, I—well, I don't know what to say," she stuttered.

"Please, say yes. You have to say yes Carrie."

"Yes, yes, I'll marry you. I can't believe you did this. " She slide the ring on her dainty finger and admired its beauty.

***

Carrie didn't waste any time planning her wedding to Terrence. She spent every waking hour planning every detail because she was only a few months away from giving birth to their daughter. It was a must she be a married woman before this would happened and she made good on that promise to herself. Two months after the wedding Carrie gave birth to a six pound baby girl, which they named MaTaysha Coleman.

Chapter Seven

Terrence marched into the oddly quiet house. "Why are you sitting there letting Taysha color all over everything?" He gathered several loose papers from the floor.

"She's fine Terrence. I gave her paper so she could draw and I could get in a little work," Carrie replied.

"It should be in one pile. Not all over the floor. Have you been sitting here all day working?"

"Oh, Daddy," Taysha cried running to her bedroom.

Carrie stood. "What the hell is your problem? How many times do I have to tell you not to do that in front of her? If you have a problem with anything I do, pull me aside. Taysha's beginning to feel like all this arguing is her fault and that's not cool Terrence. You shouldn't take your attitude out on us because someone outside this house has pissed you off." She removed her glasses.

"Here you go with this mess again." Terrence waved her off.

Carrie spoke in a low tone. "You're dang right, here I go again and you're going to keep hearing my mouth until these unknown calls stop. All the hang ups and the dead silence when I do answer are too much to handle. I can't take it anymore."

"How am I supposed to know who's calling?" Terrence screamed.

"Don't underestimate my intelligence. If you want this low self-esteem chick you know that door swings both ways. I'm not holding you here. Now, if you'll excuse me, I'm going to check on our daughter." Carrie pushed past Terrence.

"Carrie stop. Please, come here for a second."

"What could you possibly want to say right now? I'm beyond pissed at you."

"Listen to me Carrie. There is no other woman other than you in my life. I have changed everything about me for you. I'm willing to do whatever it takes to keep our family together. I just need you to trust that I belong to you. No other woman could ever change that."

"I've never been a naïve woman. I do everything I can to make you happy. I'm totally invested in this family. I don't understand why you would need to go anywhere else. But, that's something you need to deal with. Those are your issues. Taysha and I will be fine with or without you, sweetheart."

"For the millionth time, woman, I'm not seeing anyone else. What can I do to make you understand that?"

"You don't need to do anything." Carrie turned down the hallway to Taysha's bedroom.

"Mommy, are we still going to Grandma's house tonight?" Taysha sat on the floor with her dolls.

"Yes, baby. Go put your shoes on." Carrie quickly went in search of her shoes as well.

"Where are you going?" Terrence grabbed her arm.

"I guess you forgot we were supposed to go to your mother's house tonight."

"Momentarily but I'm ready whenever you guys are," he replied.

"We're ready." Carrie held Taysha's hand and walked toward the garage.

Tasha Wright

Terrence ensured Taysha was buckled safely in the backseat. "Carrie, I really want to get past whatever this is we're going through. I want you to know where I stand. I love you. I love our family and I want to make things better."

"You could've fooled me because it seems you don't care about anything anymore. You run around here with this horrible attitude of yours and I've had it."

Terrence backed the truck out the driveway to begin their short drive to his mother's house. "I could say the same about you." He signaled to journey towards the highway.

"How dare you fix your lying mouth to say some mess like that to me. I've been the one holding this family together. I could have and should have left you a long time ago. You didn't just start acting like this overnight you know."

"You've been so busy trying to connect the dots to this phone mess that you forgot to be my wife. You're frigid and you're not the woman I married." He sped through the highway.

"It would behoove you to not speak about this with our child in the car."

Terrence replied, exiting off the highway. "All I'm saying is I want us to get back on track. I want you to be the woman I fell in love with."

"I can't be that woman if you're not the same man. How could I continue to give you a hundred percent when you're barely giving me fifty," Carrie asked.

Terrence parked in the driveway of his parents' house and unbuckled Taysha's seatbelt. "Taysha, go on inside. We'll be in shortly. Carrie, I'm willing to go above and beyond to be the man you need. Will you please find it in your heart to work with me?"

Carrie stepped out the truck. "I'll work with you when you come clean about this mystery woman calling my home."

Terrence's mother yelled out to the bickering couple. "Hey, you two, get in this house."

Terrence moseyed towards the house. "Hi, Mom, you look good as always. Dad, I see you're doing much better."

Taysha leaped into her grandpa's lap. "Hi, Grandpa," she sang.

Richard replied, kissing her chubby cheeks, "Hi, little one and how's my favorite daughter-in-law doing. How is it possible for you to get prettier every time I see you."

Carrie smiled. "Thank you, Dad. How's your leg feeling after that nasty fall you took?"

"Oh, I'll live. I need to stop being so darn clumsy," Richard replied.

"Oh Dad, it was an accident. It could happen to anyone of us."

Richard moved to the edge of the recliner. He admired Taysha's frilly dress. "You sure look pretty as a flower today."

Taysha leaped to the floor and twirled around to make her dress flare out. "Thank you, Grandpa. I picked it out myself."

Richard clapped. "You did an excellent job, honey."

"Thank you."

Carrie noticed Rolonda parking in the driveway. "Christopher's here Taysha."

"Chris, Chris," Taysha danced.

The two children embraced. "I missed you," he replied.

"Let's go jump on that thing." Taysha took his hand.

"What thing are you trying to jump on Taysha," Carrie asked placing her hand over her racing heart.

"The thing Grandma bought for us to play on in the backyard," Taysha replied.

"Oh, you mean the trampoline." Carrie exhaled.

"Yes, Mommy."

"Don't go anywhere else and look after your cousin Taysha," Terrence chimed in.

"I will Daddy."

Terrence turned toward Carrie. "I need to talk to you alone." He motioned for Carrie to follow him.

"We just got here and I haven't talked to Rolonda. Let's make this quick."

Terrence led Carrie into the small kitchen. "I don't want you to get upset but there's something you need to know."

"Oh, really. What would that be?" She placed her hand on her hip and tapped her foot.

"I did lie to you. I know who's calling the house."

"I knew you were lying the entire time. How could you lie to me all this time? You made me feel like I was losing my mind just to keep your lie going. How *dare* you? I can't even look at your right now." Carrie turned her back to him.

"Please, let me get this off my chest." He touched her shoulder to turn her around.

"Say what you need to say." Carrie shrugged her shoulders.

"I told you about my ex-girlfriend, Cynthia," Terrence replied.

"So, you're basically telling me that you're still seeing her."

"No, I haven't been with Cynthia and I'm not even sure how she got our number. My entire family has asked her to back off but she won't listen."

"So everyone in the other room knew about this but no one told me. You have me running around here looking like a complete idiot while they're probably whispering about me behind my back. This is so pathetic and embarrassing for me. You have no idea. How could you leave me in the dark, Terrence? How could you do this to me?" she babbled.

"You're taking it the wrong way. I was protecting you. Cynthia can get a little out of control when she doesn't get her way. I didn't want you to become tangled in her antics."

"What you need to do is let me handle her from now on."

"No, no, no," Terrence repeated. "I don't want Cynthia to come at you in the way she handles things. I know what she's capable of and you don't need to know that."

"It's too late, Terrence. I became involved when she started calling my house. She's causing problems in our marriage. Now, if you don't do anything about this I can only assume you're okay with it, and if you're okay with it then we no longer need to be together."

"I'm not okay with what she's doing but I'm not okay with you getting involved. If she hurts you, I don't know what I would do."

Carrie placed her hand on his chest. "Sweetheart, you don't get it. You'll have to leave our home if you don't get this under control. I can't keep dealing with this nonsense. I've never had this kind of drama in my life before you."

"Okay Carrie. I'll call her and ask her to meet us at the coffee shop tonight. I'll do whatever it takes. I don't want to leave and I'm not going to allow someone else to cause that to happen. We're a family and that's the way we're going to stay."

"So, you want me to go with you to meet her, right?" Carrie asked.

"Yes, you're my wife and Cynthia needs to know that. I should have listened to my family when they told me to do this months ago, but I was too afraid to tell you because I didn't think you would understand."

"Do you remember when you were upset with me for not giving you the opportunity to react to a dilemma I faced when we first met?" she asked.

Terrence replied attempting to call Cynthia. "Yes, I remember all too well."

"Hello," Cynthia answered.

"Hey, I need you to meet me tonight." Terrence asked.

"Wow, you finally managed to call me. Where do you want to meet?" she asked.

"Do you know where that Cappuccino/Espresso Café is on North Canon Drive?" Terrence rubbed Carrie's hand.

"Yes. What time should I be there?

"Is seven o'clock good for you?" Terrence asked.

"I'll be there." Cynthia disconnected the call.

"You're pretty handy with that number I see. Are you really going through with this?" Carrie asked.

Terrence tapped his watch. "I should have done this a long time ago. My family is not going to breakup over this mess with Cynthia. Let's get this over with."

"Okay, as long as she remains a lady I'll do the same. But, if she steps out of line with her mouth. I can't promise you how cordial I'll remain. Hopefully everyone will be on the same page after tonight."

The couple entered the den. "Mom, would you mind watching Taysha for a little while? There's something we need to take care of and it's no place for her."

"Of course my grand baby can stay here but is everything okay?"

"I told Carrie about Cynthia. We're going to meet her and see if we can't get this stuff under control." Terrence and Carrie strolled toward the front door.

"I must say I'm a little hurt that no one told me about this."

Rolonda ran over to Carrie. "Please don't be upset. We thought it was the best thing to do. We know how wild Cynthia can be and we didn't want you to get mixed up in her craziness."

"Seems like she can get crazy because Terrence told me the same thing."

Terrence opened the door. "You have no idea."

***

Terrence held the door open to the Café. They sat at a small table away from the other customers. Carrie's mouth dropped open when Cynthia walked into the café. She knew it was her immediately without ever seeing her before. Cynthia was tall and slender. She had long, straight black hair. Her skin tone was honey brown and she had the most amazing green eyes. It was like looking in a mirror. Cynthia sat at the table and her attention went directly to Carrie. Pointing in Carrie's direction she asked, "Who is this and why is she here?"

Carrie held her hand out to greet Cynthia. "Hello, I'm Mrs. Coleman."

"I wasn't talking to you." Cynthia pushed her hand away.

"I know you weren't but I'm talking to you."

"What is she doing here? I don't have anything to say to your new wife," Cynthia spoke.

Terrence slammed his hand on the table. "Cynthia, we both need to talk to you. Now sit down and be quiet for a minute."

"Don't yell at me Terrence. All I'm trying to do is fix our relationship. You told me you wanted that or have you changed your mind?"

"Don't play this game. I told you a long time ago we were through."

"Correction, you told me we could work things out," Cynthia argued.

"Don't do this. You've always been sneaky as hell. The same way you lied to me about cheating and getting pregnant. Now you're lying about us making our sad ass relationship work."

Cynthia moved closer to Terrence. She moved so close their lips almost touched. "Let me tell you something, Terrence Coleman. Nothing is over unless I say it's over and I'm nowhere near done with you or this bitch if she stays with you."

Carrie stood. "Cynthia, it's over. Terrence and I are married. That alone should tell you he doesn't want to be with you." She pointed at her large diamond wedding ring.

Cynthia never took her eyes away from Terrence. "I've tried other relationships, but you're the only man I would ever give my heart to," she cried.

Carrie pushed Cynthia away. "I see the game you want to play. We don't know each other very well and I feel for you, I really do. But, you're going to have to stop calling my house as of today and get the hell on with your life."

Cynthia stood face to face with Carrie. "I won't apologize for the phone thing, and just to let you know, I won't stop trying to pursue the love of my life. I always get what I want and that happens to be this man right here. Now, whether or not he admits it he knows he wants to be with me just as much if not more. He has told me on several occasions how much he loves me and wants me in his life."

Terrence rubbed his forehead. "Cynthia, I *don't* want you anymore. We're *over*. Go find someone who wants to be with you. You need to stop this shit. Don't call my house and don't fuck with me or my family. I personally don't enjoy being fucked with so, end this shit now."

Cynthia's eyes filled with tears. "When have you ever fixed your mouth to talk to me so disrespectful? You know I can't handle anyone talking to me like this. I love you. I was everything for you. I was your maid, your whore, whatever you wanted me to be. I was that for you."

"I'm not going to lie. You were all that to me. But I wasn't the only man you were all those things for. I wanted you to be my lady. Not every man's freak."

"Why do you keep bringing that shit up? I made one mistake with one man. Stop talking like I was with hundreds of men!"

Terrence pushed away from the table. "Carrie, let's go."

Cynthia grabbed Terrence's shirt as they tried to pass. "Please don't go. I need you. I love you and I'll never stop loving you."

"You just think you need me. Take care of yourself Cynthia." With that, Terrence and Carrie disappeared from the café.

Carrie sat inside the truck. "Whoa, that was intense. Do you think she's going to be okay?"

"You are the only woman I know who could go through something like this and ask if the other woman is okay." Terrence shook his head.

"I can't help it if I have a heart. It looks like she's desperate and in my line of business I know how things can happen when someone becomes desperate."

"Let's go pick up our baby girl and go home."

***

The next morning Carrie sat in her office at work and thought about the meeting with Cynthia. She wondered how innocent or guilty Terrence was and how strongly Cynthia was holding on to him, to them. She was snapped out of her daydream by a knock on her door. "Mrs. Coleman, there's someone here to see you," the receptionist whispered.

"I'm not expecting anyone. Do you this person's name?" Carrie asked.

"She said her name was Cynthia McRynalds."

Carrie motioned for Debra to step into her office. "What does she want?"

"She wouldn't tell me anything. She said it was personal."

"Go ahead and send her in, but if you hear voices elevate, call security immediately."

Debra nodded and motioned for Cynthia to enter the office. "I'll be right outside if you need me. Mrs. Coleman will see you now."

"Thank you, Debra. Hello Cynthia. Please, have a seat. What brought you here today?"

"I thought we could talk woman-to-woman." Cynthia sat her purse on the floor beside the chair.

"I'm always up for a friendly chat but what more could we possibly have to talk about?" Carrie asked.

"Terrence or course; what else would we talk about?" Cynthia smirked.

"I'd like for you to leave if you're here to be spiteful and rude."

"No please, I apologize. I want you to know you shouldn't fool yourself into believing Terrence doesn't love me. He'll always love me."

"You really walked in here to say that to me? Wow, you really put your balls to the wall with this move." Carrie asked.

"Terrence and I were together for seven years. How could a love like that just suddenly fade away with no feelings at all?"

"From what I've heard his feelings didn't just go away overnight. They faded over time. You know, when you were out cheating on him," Carrie replied.

"How would know what I did? Did Terrence tell you that lie?" Cynthia laughed.

"Honey, Terrence and I don't sit around and talk about you. I listen and observe. So, I know your story and all the gory details of your failed life together."

Cynthia rubbed her hands on her long legs. She adjusted her shirt. "I don't believe that for one second. Have you ever been in love with someone other than Terrence?"

"Of course I have. What kind of question is that?" Carrie fidgeted with the papers on her desk.

"Did you still love for your ex after you broke up?" Cynthia asked.

"My story isn't going to help you in the slightest way." Carrie removed her reading glasses.

"The point is, I love Terrence and I can't turn my feelings off because there's an obstacle in the way. And you my dear, are the obstacle in my way. I always do whatever I need to do in order to move an obstacle out of my way, just so you know."

"You're empty threats don't move me. But, don't you think if Terrence wanted to be with you, he wouldn't have married me."

Cynthia sighed, "I still don't understand why he did that shit. I can't seem to put the pieces together."

"I can't tell you who to love. I can't tell you what's in your heart. But, why would you want to love someone who's not showing you any love or respect? You're being your own worst enemy here," Carrie replied.

"I just came to tell you in person that I'm sorry about the phone antics but I love Terrence. I don't know how to let him go and I don't think I ever will."

"May I ask you a question?"

"Go ahead."

"If you love Terrence as much as you say you do, then why did you cheat on him?"

"I wasn't thinking about what I had until I lost him."

"When I met Terrence he expressed how much he wanted someone to love and appreciate him for who he was, and I have done that which is why I'm Mrs. Coleman. Maybe you should take this as a lesson learned."

"I did appreciate Terrence. You don't know what was going on in our relationship to keep making these comments and innuendos about us."

"Maybe I don't know everything but I do know when someone is stuck on stupid. Where do you work Cynthia?" Carrie propped her elbows on her desk.

"I'm a dance instructor at West Coast University," Cynthia answered.

"Do you enjoy what you're doing at the university?"

"I love it. It's the only thing that makes me feel alive without Terrence in my life." Cynthia crossed her legs.

"You should focus on that and stop worrying about Terrence. He's very well taken care of by me and he seems to be content with that. You need to worry about yourself."

"Is that so? Well, thank you for your time. I'll be going now," Cynthia replied grabbing her purse.

"Sure, I wish you the best."

Cynthia stood in the doorway. "I guess this will be goodbye for now."

"One could only hope," Carrie replied.

Cynthia smirked and closed the door. Her visit was strange, but Carrie had way too much to do than to sit and wonder what it all meant. She rolled her sleeves up to complete her research for her latest case. Carrie became so wrapped up in her work, she hadn't realized the time. She stood from her desk, grabbed her purse, and turned the lights off in her office.

Debra noticed a frenzy Carrie rushing out. "Is everything okay?"

"Yes, everything's fine. I really appreciate you being discreet about Cynthia. I don't need this to get out in the office."

"Oh, most definitely. Are you gone for the day," Debra asked.

"Yes, you can take the rest of the day off as well."

"Oh, wow, thank you. I'll see you tomorrow." Debra grabbed the few folders from her desk and locked them away.

Carrie jetted out the building to her car and began her journey across town. She hurried down the highway to Terrence's office where he stood outside by the glass doors visibly angry. "I'm sorry I'm late. I had so much work to do and I lost track of time," Carrie said.

"I was just about to call you. It's late and we need to pick up Taysha."

Carrie moved over to allow Terrence to drive. "I said I was sorry, okay? You really need to get your car out of the shop as soon as possible so we don't have to keep doing this."

"You're so damn self-absorbed, Carrie. There had to be a moment in that head of yours when you thought about something other than your damn work. I understand your need to grow more in your career, but you have a family. Now, I'm all for you going after your goals but don't lose sight of the things in your life that really matter. You're a married woman with a child for *Christ's* sakes." Terrence continued his rant.

"Would you just slow down and please let it go?" Carrie said, as she held on to the handle above her head.

"I'm tired of this, Carrie. You need to make more time for *us*."

"When we met you said you would understand my career meant a lot to me. I guess that was just something you felt you needed to say at the time."

"Shut up, okay. I've been very patient with you. Except when you forget you have a family. That's when I could care less about your damn job," Terrence replied exiting the highway.

"I have never forgotten what I am to you guys and you need to back off Terrence. I think I do pretty dang well balancing my life with you and Taysha with my career."

Terrence shook his head. "You always put your work ahead of everything. Today is a perfect example of just how well you balance your life."

When they arrived at Rolonda's house, there were several police cars parked in front of the house, some with lights still flashing, and yellow police tape around the perimeter of the house. Carrie pointed. "What the heck is going on around here? Have you talked to Rolonda?" she asked, bolting out the car behind Terrence.

"Excuse me, but you all cannot pass this line." An officer held out his hands.

"You have no right to not allow me through. This is my sister's house and my daughter is inside."

A neighbor pushed her way through the crowd. "Terrence, I called the police. I heard loud screaming and gunshots in the house. I don't know what's going on."

Carrie enraged, fought her way through the police line. "Get *away* from me. Don't *touch* me. Where is my daughter?" she screamed.

An emergency technician stopped. "Who is your daughter ma'am?"

"MaTaysha Coleman. She's six years old and alone. Please tell me where my daughter is right now."

"There's a little girl we just placed in the back of the ambulance but she won't talk." The emergency technician hurried to the ambulance.

Carrie shrieked, covering her mouth with her trembling hands. "Oh, my God Taysha. Mommy's here baby."

"Mommy." Taysha sat up on the stretcher revealing lacerations on her arms and legs.

"Baby girl, what happened to you?" Carrie embraced her shivering daughter.

***

Terrence reached out to a passing officer. "This is my sister's house and I need to get in there. She's a single mom and all she has is me."

"Okay sir, I'll grab the lead detective and let him know who you are."

Terrence nodded and turned to the frantic neighbor. "Mrs. Belton, did you see who left the house? Did you see anything at all?"

"No, I didn't see anyone, honey. Once all the loud commotion stopped"— she paused—"I haven't heard anything more."

The detective walked up holding a small notepad. "I was advised you know the victims."

"Please, cut the bull and tell me what's going on with my family."

"Okay, get your bearings together and follow me." The detective led him through the crowd into a house filled with people taking photos of its disarray.

"Detective, I've never been good at playing games. Tell me where my family is and I don't want to hear anything else other than that."

"Sir, I've been a detective for years and this is never easy. I need you to look at these two photos and tell me who these people are by name."

Terrence pointed at each picture. "This is my sister, Rolonda, and my nephew, Christopher."

"Okay, now take a look here," the detective said holding up the edge of the sheets covering the two lifeless bodies on the floor. "Are these the same people you just identified in the photographs?"

Terrence kneeled to the floor and embraced Rolonda. "Yes, this is my baby sister and nephew. I don't understand. Who would do this? She's never had an enemy or anyone who didn't care for her." He rubbed Christopher's arm.

The detective spoke aloud. "Please, could you give this gentleman one second of privacy with his family? I'll do all I can to find out who did this to them."

"There was a little girl here. Where is she?" Terrence asked.

"I was told her mother went to the hospital with her. She had really deep lacerations from the blows she sustained."

"She's my daughter, Detective. I think the person you need to look for is Ronald Thompson."

"Wait, they told me you name was Terrence Coleman?" the detective jotted down notes.

"Yes, that's me."

"It all makes sense now. You had a run in with Ronald and he shot you a while back. After Ronald was released on bail, we could never find him."

"I can't express to you in words what I'm feeling right now. I can't understand how someone could do this."

"Please, give us a chance to handle this. It would not in your best interest to play the vigilante. I need to get on this lead while it's hot. You and your family have my deepest condolences. Here's my card and the other officers and detectives will be here most likely for a very long time tonight. Don't hesitate to call me if you need anything." He bolted out the house.

Terrence cried watching the coroner take his sister and nephew out of the house. He sat in a chair next to the doorway. "Excuse me sir," a tall officer approached Terrence.

"Yes," he replied.

"The technician said your wife went to the hospital with your daughter."

"Oh my gosh, how's my daughter? Is she okay? Is she badly hurt?"

"She's pretty banged up but she'll be fine. By the looks of things, I can say without a doubt she's a very blessed little girl to make it out alive. She has a purpose and you should get to her as soon as you gather your thoughts."

"Yes, thank you officer," Terrence said punching the small numbers on his cell phone.

"Hello," Carrie answered.

"Is Taysha okay?"

"She's going to be fine. Don't you worry about her. I want to know how you're doing. The emergency team told me what happened to Rolonda and Christopher. I don't know what to say. I'm so sorry baby."

"I feel numb all over. I keep praying this is just a nightmare and I'll wake up any moment."

"Baby, I'm praying for you. I think you should go home and take a shower and get yourself relaxed as much as possible. I'll call your parents but I want you to go home right now, okay," Carrie said.

"I'm leaving now. They just took Rolonda and Christopher out so there's nothing else I can do here. This is just unbelievable." Terrence cried uncontrollably.

"I know it is baby but you need to get your thoughts together so you will have a safe drive home. Taysha and I will be on our way home as soon as they let her go." Carrie ended the call.

***

After another hour Carrie and Taysha were released from the hospital. She paid the cab driver and carried a sleeping Taysha in the house. "Hey sweetie, we're home," she whispered.

"How is she doing?" Terrence kissed Taysha's forehead and followed Carrie to Taysha's bedroom.

"She'll be better, physically, in no time, but of course there's no idea how soon she'll recover mentally." She tucked Taysha in bed "How are you dealing with all of this?"

Terrence followed Carrie into their bedroom with red bloodshot eyes. "I could never understand what you're feeling, but I want you to know I'm here for you."

"Thank you." His tears returned with a vengeance.

"Oh, baby, I'm going to be here for you. Taysha's hurting. She saw things no one should ever see especially, a little girl. She really needs to hear you say this wasn't her fault. She's so afraid you're upset with her, because she couldn't stop crying. That's how Ronald found them hiding, because she couldn't stop crying."

"I didn't know that. I'll talk to her in the morning."

Chapter Eight

Carrie pushed the stack of files away to answer her receptionist line. "Yes, Debra."

"Sorry to bother you but I have Ms. Delray on the phone calling for you."

"That's actually kind of perfect. Send her through."

"Carrie, hey, how are you doing?" Janitta asked.

"Well, you know what we've been dealing with. So, right now, I'm as good as I can get."

"I know honey, I know. Ronald never ceases to amaze me. Had I known he would be this destructive I wouldn't have ever entertained him this long. I knew he had a thing for you but not this strong. How's Terrence and his family?"

"Everyone's slowly coming around. They are finally accepting the fact that Rolonda and Christopher are gone."

"Gosh, I don't know how you all are still sane. What about Ronald? I think I saw something in the paper about him."

"Well, he has a preliminary hearing scheduled. The prosecutors want to pursue the death penalty because of the severity of his crime. You know once children get involved the consideration of anything other than the death penalty is pretty much out the window. They may not always get it but at some time it is sought."

"Good, he shouldn't be allowed to hurt anyone else. How's my little God daughter doing? It broke my heart to see her after all that happened. She wasn't her happy self."

"Oh, my baby is as strong as they make them. My sister agreed to keep her for a while. So, I know that's going to help her get back to herself fairly quickly."

"I guess having a psychiatrist in the family is good after all. I just wish there wasn't a need for it if that meant my little angel had to experience this craziness. Where is Terrence?"

"He went to the hearing. You know anytime they have Ronald scheduled for anything come hell or high water, Terrence makes sure he's there."

"I don't blame him. That was his only sister and her only child. Ronald is just demented and full of the devil and his evil ways. I mean, who thinks about doing something like that and actually goes through with it?"

"Yes, he's been on edge. I don't know what to do but let him go through it in his own time. I don't want to push him too fast, you know."

Terrence stormed into the office. "If you don't want whoever is on the phone to hear what I have to say I suggest you hang up now."

"Umm, Janitta. I need to call you back. What is it Terrence?" she quickly ended her call.

"Why didn't you tell me your firm took Ronald's case? Do you realize he may never pay for what he did to my family?"

Carrie stood. "I had no idea we took Ronald's case. There's no way my partner would take his case knowing what he did to our family. Wait here one second. I'll find out what's going on."

"You do that." Terrence sat down.

Carrie closed the door and walked over to her receptionist. "Do you know if Kathy's busy?" she whispered.

"No, she's with a client. Is something wrong? Could I help?"

"Do you know anything about our firm taking Ronald Thompson's case?" Carrie asked.

"No, that's what I've been trying to tell you all morning. There has been a huge mix up. Another law firm took his case. But, I don't think you want to know who took the case, even though I feel you should."

"Look, I have a pissed off husband in my office about to blow his top. Just spit it out."

"Davion has Ronald's case." She grabbed a small piece of paper from her top drawer.

"I can't believe he would do that. He just moved back and already he's causing turmoil. I need you to get the address to his office as soon as possible for me, please."

Debra handed Carrie the small piece of paper. "I'm way ahead of you. It's downtown on Lexington Drive. Good luck."

Carrie turned to enter her office. "Thanks Debra." She closed the door. "Terrence, I need to tell you something but I don't want you to get upset with me. I had no idea about this."

"So, your damn partner took his case, didn't she? I should go give her a piece of my damn mind."

"No, my firm doesn't have Ronald's case. Davion took it." She closed her eyes.

"You have got to be kidding me. That jackass can't do this to us."

"I'll get to the bottom of this. You go home and let me deal with it. Go check up on Taysha at your mom's house before she leaves today. My sister is flying out to take her home for a while."

"Why didn't you tell me you were sending her to Washington?" Terrence asked.

"I didn't want to bother you too much. I know you're still up in the air with all that's going on. Besides, I thought it would be good for Stephanie to talk to her and figure out where her mind is these days."

"I wish you wouldn't do things behind my back. I'm there every day with you and Taysha, and you take it upon yourself to do something like this. I'll go see her off, but damn Carrie, I didn't want her to go, especially after everything she's gone through with Ronald. I just feel like we should all stay together so I will know everyone's okay." Terrence stood to depart.

Carrie grabbed her purse and followed Terrence out of the office. "You don't understand how hard it is for me to be there with the both of you. You lost your sister and nephew and Taysha actually witnessed that loss. I can't deal with you two at the same time. I need help okay? So, if my sister has offered me help, you're dang right I'm going to accept it." She disarmed her alarm and threw her purse inside.

"You don't get it. I'll go over and take Taysha to the Airport to meet Stephanie. You just see about your ex and find out why in the hell he would take this case knowing your only child was involved." He cranked his truck.

Carrie sat in her car and typed Davion's address into her GPS. She practiced what she would say in order to maintain her composure on her drive over.

***

Carrie stepped out her car and took a deep breath. She swung the door open to Davion's small building. "I need to speak with Mr. Hewitt."

"What is your name, ma'am?" the receptionist asked.

"Carrie Johnson. I'm sure he's expecting me."

The receptionist spoke into the phone. "Mr. Hewitt, there's a Carrie Johnson here to speak with you."

"Yes, send her in," Davion replied.

"Right this way, Ms. Johnson." The receptionist stood.

"Hello there, Mrs. Coleman, how are you doing?" Davion smiled and kissed Carrie's cheek.

Carrie pushed Davion away. "Wipe that smug grin off your face Davion. You know why I'm here. We need to talk."

"What could be so important that you would drive downtown instead of picking up the phone to talk to me?"

"Why did you take Ronald's case?" Carrie spoke.

"Oh, so we're getting straight to the point I see. Well, business is business. Ronald is my client and I'm going to do my best to get him a fair trial."

"You know he's guilty. He hurt my child. How could you do this to me? You're digging your own grave. You're starting a new law firm, for goodness sake."

"What makes you so sure I'm digging my grave? Were you at the scene of the crime as it was taking place? My client is innocent until proven guilty."

Carrie stood by the door. "No, I wasn't there, but my daughter was." She wiped the stream of tears from her eyes.

Davion walked over to Carrie and placed his arm around her. "Wait a minute. I want to make you an offer."

"So, you're going to bargain with me over something this morbid and sick." She took a deep breath.

"I'm not bargaining. I need time alone with you and I'm willing to drop the case. There's just one thing I want you to do for me."

"What could that possibly be?" Carrie crossed her arms over her chest.

"I want you to spend one night with me. If you can do that I'll take myself off the case. Ronald reached out to me and I've done what I could and I think you know how convincing I can be. However, if I drop the case his sentence would still stand."

"Davion, this is too sick. This is not you. How could you even think to come to me with something like this? I need to go."

"So, you'll think about it," he asked.

"Jackass." Carrie stormed out of the tiny office.

"Wear something sexy," Davion laughed.

Carrie hurried to her car to place a call. "Hello," Janitta answered.

"Dang Janitta, the phone only rang once. Are you expecting a call?"

"I thought you were my ex-fiancé," she replied.

"What happened this time?" Carrie sat in the congested downtown traffic.

"William dumped me. He said things were not going the way he planned and that he'd fallen in love with someone else. He said I wasn't the woman I used to be. I haven't heard from him since he gave that little speech two days ago," Janitta ranted.

"Watch where you're going, you dumb ass," Carrie screamed at a driver who cut her off. "Sorry about that. What are you going to do?"

"What else can I do besides move the heck on? He clearly doesn't want to be with me."

"Well, if you need someone to talk to, you know I'm always a phone call away. As a matter of fact, why haven't you called me? Lord knows you worship the ground that man walks on."

"You've been dealing with your own drama. I didn't want to put you into overload with my trivial problems."

"I know how to cope with stress. My job taught me that. I called you because I need your advice."

"Anything to get my mind off William. What's up," Janitta asked.

"You know the entire ordeal with Ronald."

"Unfortunately, yes. What did he do now?" Janitta asked.

"Well, due to him gaining legal representation he dropped the court appointed attorney. So, this attorney is trying to get the death sentence dropped."

"Who in their right mind would touch that case?"

"None other than the infamous Davion Hewitt," Carrie replied.

"You're joking right? When did Davion take the bar exam? As far as I know he went to law school but never attempted to pass the bar."

"He did that a few years ago, before he moved. I went to his office and had a talk with him just now."

"Damn, Carrie, you're circling the airport. Bring it in," Janitta shrieked.

"He said he would drop the case if I would spend one night with him."

"That's low. That doesn't sound like him. Why would he do that knowing your daughter was hurt? You need to think about how that would affect your family before you do something like that."

"I know what you're saying, but there's a part of me that really wants to do this. You don't see how Terrence is now. He walks around like a zombie. If Davion were to get Ronald off, I don't think Terrence would get over it."

"If you go through with this, how will you keep it quiet?" Janitta asked.

"I haven't thought about the details. That's why I'm calling you to help me with this. I want to do this for Terrence because I see how this is taking over him and I want my husband back."

"I'm your best friend and I support you in whatever you decide to do but part of me tells me you want to do this for your own personal reasons."

"You think I want to be with Davion?" She asked.

"I think you're still in love with him. This is an easy excuse for you to be with him. You're starting to act like your Aunt Jackie. She's had men lined up for years."

"Oh, don't say that. But, I have to admit I'm confused. I love both Terrence and Davion in different ways. I love Terrence because he gave me the family I've always wanted but I can't let Davion go in my heart. Even though he's acting like an evil jackass. Terrence does play second to Davion in my heart and he always has." She exited the highway.

"It's nice to hear you finally admit it. I've known from day one. I'm here for you but I can't make this decision for you Carrie. This is something you'll have to do on your own. I don't think I could handle knowing anything about it," Janitta admitted.

"This is difficult." Carrie ended the call but found herself driving toward Janitta's studio.

"What are you doing here? I thought we just hung up?" Janitta said, running toward the parking lot.

"I know but I still have no idea what I'm going to do." Carrie followed Janitta inside her studio.

"Have a seat and take a breath. Tell me what you think will happen if you don't go through with this."

"Ronald could get away with what he did. My daughter will never have justice and Terrence will probably lose his mind."

"Do you truly believe Davion will keep his word and drop the case? I personally feel like he's just trying to do whatever he can to get your attention."

"Do you think that's what he's doing?" Carrie asked.

"Yes, I don't see Davion doing this to you. He loves you too much."

"I still can't risk it. I'm going to call him and tell him I'll do it."

Janitta frowned. "I don't want to risk sounding redundant, but be mindful of the choices you make."

Chapter Nine

Carrie dressed in a short black cocktail dress. "Hey honey." Carrie replied putting on her make-up.

"How late are you and Janitta planning on hanging out tonight?" Terrence asked.

"I don't know. We just need a little girl time." She fluffed her curls.

"It's lonely here with Taysha gone, and now you're leaving me, too."

"If you don't want me to go, just say the word."

"No, you made your point earlier. You need a break from me and Taysha. I get it."

"I won't stay out too late." Carrie put on her black heels and walked out to her jeep. She drove to the address Davion gave her when she decided to take him up on his offer.

Davion stood by the door to the dark building. "Hey, sexy, I love this dress."

"Let's get this over with." Carrie allowed Davion to help her out her car.

"Are you going to have this attitude all night Carebear?" Davion replied.

"Why are we here? This place is dark and deserted."

"You'll see, baby face." He held the door open for Carrie.

"Please don't try to have sex with me." She shook her finger.

"Sex is the last thing on my mind. I wouldn't disrespect you like that. You had a choice and you decided to be here with me so, I know you really want to be here. Relax and enjoy yourself."

Carrie tugged on the hem of her dress as she followed Davion into the candle-lit Japanese eatery. She saw two oversized silk pillows sitting below a table that sat close to the floor. The table was filled with small teacup candles. The appetizers were already on the table along with wine.

"What do you think," Davion asked.

"This was the dinner we shared the last night you were in LA, right?" Carrie asked.

"Yes, you remembered. Do you still want to go home?" he asked.

"Not right now, but don't ruin the moment thinking with your little head. How did you get the owner to do this for you?" She reached for the appetizers.

"He's a friend of mine. I wanted to do something special for you."

"I'm not going to sit here and pretend I'm okay with the tactics you used to get me here. How could you stoop so low?"

"I never planned on trying Ronald's case. I know it was a low blow and I know it was a stupid in- humane thing to do. But, I needed to figure out a way to get you to listen to me. I need you to see that I'm still the man for you." He took a bite of his food the waiter placed on the table.

"I'm married. You can't put me in this type of position."

The waiter removed the empty appetizer platter and excused himself. "I needed a chance to plead my case to you. I'm not asking you to leave your husband. I just want you to hear what I have to say."

"You sure need to say a lot now that you're here but you never said a word to me when you were away. So, make sure you say what you need to say right now, because this it. We can't keep doing all this sneaking around every time you feel the need to talk to me. That's why we have phones genius." Carrie placed a white cloth napkin across her lap and began eating her dinner.

"I love you with all my heart. If I knew this is where we would be in our relationship, I would have never left with my company. Now that I've had to live without you in my life. I realize how stupid I was to leave you. I would do anything to get you back but I know you're married now. I just want you to know how deep you're still in my heart and how much I love you," Davion said.

"You went an entire year without calling me once. How can you sit there and say you love me?" Carrie replied.

"To be honest, it would've hurt me more to hear your voice and know that I couldn't touch you or hold you. But, it's killing me to know another man is holding you." He held her hands.

"If you had been honest about your feelings a long time ago maybe we could have salvaged what we had but you decided to let it go, and I have to let you go."

"Carrie, moving away hurt me more than I could ever express to you in words. I never meant to hurt you. You mean the world to me and I'll never understand why I made the decision to move away. My mind was jaded, chasing dollar signs. I was wrong for putting my career before you and asking you to forget about your dreams. I can honestly tell you my feelings will never change. You'll always have my heart," Davion confessed.

"I'll always love you but you know we could never get back what we had. Too much time has passed and I have a child now. It's crazy because I could never understand how a person could say they love more than one person at a time but that's just the way I feel. I can't understand how you can be in my heart so dang deep I can't think straight."

"I feel the same way about you. My love for you will never change. I don't wish anything bad with your marriage but if Terrence slips up, I want you to know I'll always be here. Did you enjoy your dinner?" Davion asked.

"Yes, it was perfect. Be sure to thank the chef for me. As always, you've out done yourself."

"Are you ready to go?" He helped Carrie to her feet.

"So, this is it. You don't have anything else planned." She placed the napkin over her plate.

"I told you all I wanted to do was tell you how I felt and I've done that," Davion assured his lovely companion.

Carrie replied, walking hand in hand with Davion to her car, "I'm surprised you didn't want to do more."

"I respect the fact that you belong to someone else now. I think you're the kind of woman any man would love to spend the rest of his life catering to. I know that's why Terrence claimed you as his wife so quickly. I don't want you to feel bad about any of your decisions. You have to do what makes you happy. I failed to be the man you needed and you found a man who was more than willing to fill that spot. That's my loss baby girl."

"Wow, I guess this is grown up talk." Carrie started her engine.

"Good-bye sweetheart." Davion bent over to kiss Carrie for the last time.

Carrie peered through her rearview mirror until she could no longer see Davion. She weaved in and out of traffic until she reached her humble abode. Carrie parked in the garage and looked at her puffy eyes in the vanity mirror before tiptoeing through the house to her bedroom. Carrie sat by the bay window in her bedroom and stared into the stars and space. Her mind wouldn't stop thinking about Davion and his confessions to her.

Terrence rolled over in the bed to talk to Carrie. "How long have you been sitting here in the dark crying?"

"I'm sorry. Did I wake you?"

"Don't worry about that. Tell me why you were crying."

"I'll be fine honey." Carrie removed her heels.

"Whatever is bothering you. I'm here for you if you would like to talk about it," Terrence assured her.

"No, no, I'm sure it's nothing. I've just had a really long day and I'm worn out. I should've stayed home with you tonight baby." Carrie changed into her gown.

"Come to bed ."

Carrie couldn't sleep. She had too much on mind and it was running a mile a minute throughout the night.

***

Terrence blocked his eyes from the sunlight. "Good morning baby. Did you get any sleep last night?"

Carrie sat on the side of the bed with her back to Terrence. "No. Not much at all," she replied.

"Carrie talk to me. What's on your mind so heavy that you can't sleep?" Terrence pleaded.

"You have bigger problems to deal with other than my issues. I can get through this on my own."

"Carrie, I thought you said you wouldn't hold this Cynthia thing against me. You obviously still have a problem with it. I can't think of anything else that would keep you up all night."

"I'm not thinking about Cynthia. I will be fine." Carrie walked away to take a shower.

Terrence, followed behind Carrie still ranting. "Hey, hold on. Talk to me." He grabbed her arm.

Carrie freed her arm from Terrence's grip. "Don't you ever man handle me like that. I said I can handle it. Leave it alone, baby."

Terrence stared at a woman who looked like his wife but her words and actions were spoken as a complete stranger. "Okay, okay. I'll let it go." He backed away.

Carrie stepped into the bathroom and locked the door. After her shower she dressed she headed to her car and turned on the radio. The news station announced the radical change of events that Ronald no longer had an attorney. Davion kept his word and took himself off the case. Carrie felt the urge to thank him. Something in her heart wouldn't allow her to let him go. She backed out of her garage and headed to his office to thank him. Only, on her drive over she could feel something changing inside her. She was already beginning to rekindle feelings for Davion. Carrie stepped out of her car and headed into the office where the receptionist allowed her through immediately. "I want to thank you for keeping your end of the deal." She stood in front of Davion in his small office.

"I told you I would never do that to you. I needed more time with you Carebear. I wanted you to know how I felt and now that you do, I won't bother you anymore."

"My feelings for you have never changed. But you have hurt me more than you could ever imagine."

"I hurt myself just as bad. Do you realize you were the best thing that's ever happened to me? You were made for me and I'm afraid I'll never find that again." Davion pouted.

"You're the most compassionate man I've ever known. You will eventually find a woman to settle down with and she'll love you just as much as I do or more because you're that kind of man."

"I love you." Davion took Carrie in his arms, and embraced her.

She looked up at him. Something about his eyes always burned into her soul. "I want to stay with you tonight."

"What about your family?" He held her tighter in his arms.

"Let me deal with that. I want to be with you tonight."

"Why are you changing your mind now," Davion asked.

"I need to be near you, but if you don't want me to stay then I'll have no choice but to understand."

"I would love nothing more than to be near you once again. But, I don't want you to put yourself in a bad situation because of me. Beside, you know if you stay the night with me, I'll want to feel that part of you all night long."

"What part of me," Carrie asked.

"Don't act like you don't know what I'm talking about." Davion laughed.

"I don't know," Carrie glowed.

Davion kissed the nape of her neck. "I want to explore you inside out baby. I want to make love to you."

"I would love that. How about I go home and come over to your place in a few hours."

"I'll see you then." They shared a long kiss. Davion scribbled his address on the back of his business card.

"Oh, hey, this is the neighborhood we were thinking about buying a house before you moved, wasn't it?"

"Yes, I always said, if I ever came back to L.A. that's where I would buy my house."

"That's so sweet. I love everything about you. I do miss you a lot Davion."

"All you have to do is say the word and I'll forever be yours," Davion replied.

"Slow down baby," Carrie giggled walking out the office. She smiled all the way home. There would be no if and or buts about her staying with Davion. It was going to happen that night. She wore the biggest smile she'd had in a very long time. Traffic didn't even bother her. She sat in her car for another moment before going inside. She waited long enough to wipe the smile off her face. She bounced upstairs to see Terrence packing. "Where are you going?" she asked.

"I told you days ago I had a meeting in Ohio. The offer still stands for you to come with me if you want."

"I wish I could, but I have a lot of work tomorrow."

"Call me if you need me. I love you and I'll call you when I land."

"I love you too," Carrie replied.

Terrence snapped his fingers. "Oh, hey, Are you ready to tell me what's on your mind?"

"What do you mean?"

"Last night, I could tell you had something on your mind. Was it about us?" he asked.

"Oh no, it didn't have anything to do with the two of us. We're okay sweetie."

"Do you want to talk about whatever it is?" Terrence asked.

"No, I'll sort it out on my own. Thank you for caring."

"I don't want to push you, but if you change your mind I'm all ears." Terrence descended downstairs.

"Thank you, have a safe flight."

Carrie walked Terrence to the door. She peeped out the window for a few minutes until Terrence disappeared down the street then she ran upstairs and grabbed her tan overnight bag. Carrie jetted out the house with her overnight bag in hand. She wasted no time rushing over to Davion's house. She was in such a hurry to see him she ran to the door and rang the doorbell as quickly as she could.

"It's open," Davion yelled from the kitchen.

She entered and looked around. "Where are you?"

"Hey Carebear, I'm in the kitchen."

Carrie fanned her face as she neared the kitchen. "What's with all the smoke?" She covered her nose.

"Is that the thanks I get for trying to cook for your behind? I'm making your favorite. Fried chicken a la Davion," He laughed.

"I appreciate you for thinking of me, my Nubian King." She wrapped her arms around his waist.

"See, that's what I love about you. I can't name one woman who always tells her man she appreciates everything he does for her."

"I give credit where credit is due."

Davion turned and cuddled with Carrie in his arms. "You're so amazing."

"I think I'll go take a long bubble bath while you finish up."

"I see you still take fifty baths a day. Make yourself at home baby."

Carrie stopped walking up the staircase. "I just had a thought."

"Should I be afraid to ask?" Davion replied.

"I was thinking you could join me."

Davion quickly turned the fire off on the gas stove. "I'm right behind you. Let me put this stuff away and I'll be right there."

"Which bathroom should I use?" She looked around.

"Use the one in my bedroom upstairs. It's the fourth door on your right."

"Hurry and get up here," She took her shirt off and continued up the stairs.

"Do you want me to bring champagne?" Davion asked.

Carrie slide her skirt off and kept walking. "Just bring yourself. We don't need any help. We never did," she laughed.

Davion walked into the bathroom and dimmed the lights. He removed his clothes and joined Carrie in the warm bath. Carrie turned and straddled him, planting soft kisses on his smooth chest. "I love how you never grow hair on your chest. I miss you and me doing simple things like this together."

"I do, too, baby." Davion closed his eyes.

Carrie squeezed the water from the bath sponge onto Davion's back. "You're still so sexy to me. I love everything about you."

"Thank you, sweetheart." He kissed her neck.

Carrie stepped out of the bath and grabbed a large blue towel to dry herself off. She walked into the bedroom and positioned herself on top of the king-size bed. "Come here, baby."

Davion rose to her request in more ways than one. He climbed onto the bed and gave his sweetheart a passionate kiss as he nibbled her bottom lip. Carrie moaned. Passion filled every inch of her body, She reached her hand out to massage his rigid manhood. He held his head back and moved his hips to her hand motions. Carrie grew excited as she watched his pleasure grow.

"I miss you, Carrie."

She kissed his chest and buried her face in his lap and continued with the same pace. Davion gripped the top of his headboard and curled his toes so tight they cracked. Carrie could feel herself become wet. She climbed on top of Davion and slowly rode him, looking deep into his eyes. Their love-making held more passion than it ever had before. Tears fell from her eyes feeling the kisses Davion placed all over her body. Continuing to ride him, she held her head back and cupped her breasts.

Davion took control. Flipping Carrie onto her back, he thrust in and out of her hard and slow. She felt every inch of him inside her, touching her every wall. He held his eyes shut and slowly grinded until his control abandoned him, He let out a loud cry and his lover held his hips to meet his passion. She moved in a circular motion until she climaxed.

"Oh, Davion," she screamed.

He held Carrie in his arms. "I know you're not the casual sex type of woman so where does this leave us?"

"I really don't know what to make of all these emotions I'm feeling."

"Talk to me."

"I love you and I miss being with you. Don't get me wrong, I love my husband, but for some reason I can't let you go."

"So what are we going to do about this?"

"Your guess is as good as mine."

As they fell asleep they felt complete for the first time in a long time.

***

In the morning, Carrie realized she had a lot of things to consider. "Davion, I really hate to leave but I need to get to work."

"I never considered how I would feel when you would leave. Carrie, I would be so hurt if you walked out of this house to never return."

"Aww, you're already missing you're Carebear. Well, trust me. You're not the only one who feels that way baby."

"I don't know if I could handle these fly-by nights. I'm still in love with you. I need more than just a weekend of sex. I need all of you baby."

Carrie knelt over the bed to kiss her true love good-bye. "This gives me a lot to think about. It would be selfish of me to keep you hanging. I'll call you later and we can talk about this." Carrie grabbed her purse and scurried out to her car. She pushed the speed limit because she needed to get home before Terrence. When she arrived home she hurried to take a shower and spend the rest of her day in her office and began working on her case load. She hadn't realized how much time passed until she finally looked up from her work when she heard Terrence unlocking the door to enter.

"I'm home," Terrence announced, closing the door behind him.

"How was your trip?" She reached for her car keys.

"I missed you. Are you feeling better?"

"Yes, I'm better," Carrie replied.

"Would you like to join me upstairs for a while?" He ran his hand down her slender back.

"You haven't asked me that in so long I don't know what to say."

"Say you'll follow me upstairs."

"I wish I could, but I was just on my way to the office. I need to prep this case before my clients come to the office tomorrow. I need to be on my A-game."

Terrence looked at his watch. "Carrie, it's seven o'clock. Why would you possibly need to go to the office right now?"

"I just told you why I needed to go. I've been working on this case all weekend and I'm really hot. I'm making ground here."

"You'll never change honey. Could I at least drive you to your office and hang in there with you? I could try to help as much as I can without being in the way and after we could go to dinner."

"No, you just had a long flight home. Go take a shower and relax. I'll be back before you know it."

"So, in other words. When you get home you'll be in your office working through the night. Could I at least have a kiss?" Terrence asked.

Carrie replied, jingling her keys, "You know that's a given. I better go get that file baby."

Terrence shook his head. "Ah, the life of having a devoted lawyer as a spouse," he whispered and headed upstairs to call it a night.

***

The next morning Carrie was hard at work when her concentration was broken by her receptionist. "I was in a zone Debra. This better be good."

"Davion is here and he says it's really important that he speaks with you."

"By all means, send him in. Have a seat. How are you doing, sweetheart?" Carrie welcomed Davion.

"I could be better. But, this visit isn't about me." Davion held his head down.

"By the look on your face it must be pretty serious." She stepped away from her desk.

"My sister's baby was delivered stillborn the other day. My mom says she needs my help but I don't know what to say or do."

"Oh, my goodness, I'm so sorry to hear that. Why are you here with me? You should be with Felicia."

"She needs someone else to talk to her about this. Mom doesn't know how to separate her feelings to help Felicia.

This is her second stillbirth and you and Felicia have always been close. Will you come with me?" Davion asked.

"Slow down. When are you leaving?"

"I'm trying to get a flight out today. So, are you coming?" he asked.

"Of course, of course," she repeated. "I'll give you a call in a little while to let you know for sure."

"Please call me. I really need you. The family needs you."

"Give me an hour. If push comes to shove, Terrence may tag along. Is that going to be a problem?"

"I don't care about him. I just want you to be there for Felicia."

Carrie quickly gathered her things and headed home to explain why she needed to go to Montana. This time she powered the radio off on her drive home. She held her queasy stomach as she turned the corner to her home. She wasn't going to take no for an answer on this one. Her hand began to shake when she reached out to unlock her front door.

"What are you doing home so early," Terrence asked.

"Something terrible has happened. Baby, please be open minded about this."

"Go ahead." Terrence listened.

Carrie hit the magazine Terrence was reading. "Would you please put the magazine down and look at me. You never give me your undivided attention. My friend's baby was stillborn. This is the second child she's lost during birth, so she isn't taking it too well. She really needs to be surrounded by people who love her and I want to be one of those people in her time of need."

"Do I know this friend you're referring to?" Terrence asked.

"I won't lie to you. She's Davion's sister but she has been a friend to me for many years."

"Whatever, just go." Terrence shrugged.

"Are you sure?"

"Yeah, go." He grabbed the magazine to continue reading the article.

"You could come with me. I've already told him you would be coming. It's totally okay."

"You can't be serious. I don't want you to be around that smug son of a bitch. But, I won't keep you away from your friend during a time when she needs you."

"If you have a problem with me going, I won't go. I don't want to hurt you."

"I said go. I don't care." He flipped the page in the magazine.

Carrie nodded and turned to go downstairs to make a call. "Hey, stranger, what are you up to," Carrie asked.

"Nothing at all. Running on this treadmill. Where have you been?" Janitta asked out of breath.

"I need you to take a quick trip with me for a couple of days. Do you think you can get away?"

"Sure, where are we going? You know I'm always up for a trip. What's the occasion?" Janitta asked.

"Felicia had another stillbirth. She needs us J."

"Where's Mrs. Hewitt?"

"You know their mom finds it hard to console people. It's hit or miss with her."

"That, I do I remember. When do you want to go?" Janitta asked.

"In a few hours, so get your things packed and make sure you pack some sexy outfits. We still need to find you a good man."

"I second that," Janitta said.

"I'll give you call when I'm on my way to pick you up. I have another call coming in so I'll talk to you in a little while." Carrie pushed the button on her small Bluetooth earpiece to accept her other call. "Hello."

"Hey sweetie, it's Davion? What's the plan. Are you coming?"

"Everything looks good this way. What flight are you on? I need to get tickets."

"I'm on flight 128 at five o'clock. Is Terrence coming?" Davion asked.

"No, but Janitta's coming." She typed on her computer to purchase tickets.

"Wow, I haven't talked to that crazy woman in a long time."

"You should be that excited to see me," Carrie replied.

"Don't be jealous, baby, you know I love you. But, I haven't seen Janitta in a long time."

"Okay handsome. We'll see you in a little while."

"Hey, why don't you guys come to my house. I'm closer to the airport. We can share a cab."

"Sounds like a plan. I'm packing now and when I finish I'll go pick up Janitta and we will be on our way to your house from there." Carrie ran around the house stuffing everything in her luggage. She kissed Terrence goodbye and jetted out the house to race across town to get Janitta. When she turned the corner to reach Janitta's house she saw her dragging her luggage outside. Carrie couldn't believe how amazing Janitta looked. She wore a turquoise halter dress that fell on her body in all the right places. Her hair was dyed a sandy red color and cut in a short, sassy style. She sparkled of diamonds everywhere. Her earrings were diamonds. Her necklace was diamonds. She had two large diamond rings on each hand with a diamond tennis bracelet. "I see you're ready to roll. Girl you are looking way too hot for me. You have my mouth hanging wide open and I'm not even into women," Carrie joked.

"Yes, I am. I've been waiting on you. What took you so long?" Janitta asked.

Carrie circled Janitta like a hawk. "Forget that, how long has it been since I last saw you? You have totally reinvented yourself Miss Lady."

"Why thank you. I do what I can do." Janitta strutted.

"You've lost a ton of weight."

Janitta twirled to show her new figure, "Well let's not go that far. I didn't lose a ton of weight but I did lose fifty pounds. I've gotten back into my size nines."

"You look *amazing.*"

"I can't wait to see our old spot again. It's been about nine years, right?" The two women packed Janitta's two bags into the trunk of Carrie's car.

"Yeah, I think that's about how long it's been. Davion wants us to meet him at his house."

Janitta clapped her hands. "Let's go. We have to get our girl back on track bless her heart." They sang to the music as they traveled across town. Carrie felt young a free again. Like she didn't have a care in the world. She weaved in and out of traffic to reach Davion's house while Janitta spoke to customer service to ensure their tickets were squared away on the same flight as Davion.

"Are we on the same flight as Davion?" Carrie asked.

"I'll have to go on a date with Roger from the airport when I get back but he yes ma'am, he hooked us up," she laughed.

"Oh my goodness. You are too much."

"Girl, I'm just praying he isn't buck teethed and crossed eyed."

"You will never change. You are a dang good friend to take one for the team like that," Carrie giggled.

Davion ran to the truck to greet the ladies with a hug. "Hey, hey, hey. Am I going to have to break up this little reunion in order for us to make our flight? You guys can do this on the plane," Carrie said. The three quickly packed their luggage in the trunk of the cab Davion had waiting when they arrived.

"Ooh, somebody's jealous. It's written all over your face," Janitta laughed.

Carrie laughed. "Girl, Davion knows what's good for him. Where are we staying while we're in Montana," she asked.

"I thought we could just stay at my mom and dad's house. If you want to do something different, that's cool with me," Davion replied.

"That's cool with me. How about you, J?"

"You know I'm easy like Sunday morning. I can roll with whatever," Janitta replied.

Davion laughed. "So Janitta, how's the photography business treating you?"

"Everything's going great. I'm thinking of opening another studio soon."

"Look at you doing your thing. I'm proud of you. I think we're all doing very well tackling our dreams like we said we would in college." Davion shook his head.

"What dreams did you shout to the mountain tops in college? You were too busy trying to fight to prove your love to this thing over here," Janitta pointed at Carrie.

"You did used to fight a lot Davion. Anytime another guy would look in my direction you turned into a deranged animal." Carrie laughed.

"I was digging you maybe a little too much." Davion tipped the cab driver. They hurried to grab their luggage and retrieve their tickets to get through the heavy airport security.

"You guys I really need to get some sleep during the flight. I'm totally wiped out," Carrie said.

"I hear you. I'll be out before the plane takes off. I'm sure as soon as I get in my seat I'll be out like a light," Janitta replied.

Davion lead the two women to their tunnel to get ready and board their flight. "You two could never hang. I can't remember how many road trips I was stuck doing all the driving because you wanted to sleep."

"Oh, please, you didn't want anyone driving your old ugly car even if we tried," Carrie replied.

"My car was hot. I don't know what you're talking about," Davion reiterated.

"That car was not hot. I hated that car." Janitta laughed laying her head back and closing her eyes.

***

Davion tapped the two sleeping beauties as the flight attendant announced the need to prepare for landing. "Wake up, we're landing. Buckle your seat belts."

"That was fast. Seems like we just left." Carrie asked.

"Janitta, don't make that ugly just woke up face. You guys have been sleep for about an hour and forty-five minutes. That was a power nap," he laughed.

"Yeah, you just laugh it up. You won't be laughing when we're in the process of landing and you get all nervous like you always do. *Oh my God, Carrie, Carrie. It feels like the plane is falling apart,*" Carrie mocked Davion fluffing her hair.

"Trust me, I won't give you two the satisfaction of seeing me scared anymore. You never let stuff go." Davion looked down as the plane got lower and lower.

"Open your eyes man. Look out the window and see the ground form and buildings get bigger," Janitta teased.

"Stop it. I can't take it," Davion whimpered.

Carrie laughed. "You can open your eyes now. We've landed cry baby."

"That's not funny Carebear. I thought you loved me," Davion said.

"Aww, I'm sorry baby but you know whenever we fly I have a guaranteed laugh sitting next to you." They walked out with the other first class passengers to enter the airport.

Davion whispered in Carrie's ear. "I've been meaning to ask you, what have you been doing because your backside has really grown from what I remembered."

Carrie slapped his arm. "Stop it. You are so bad. But baby I've been hitting those squats like nobody's business." The trio retrieved their luggage and walked through the airport with shades on like they were true celebrities at heart.

Davion picked up the pace as they neared an area filled with vehicles. "Follow me, ladies, and let's see if my truck is here."

"What kind of truck did you rent?" Janitta asked.

Davion disarmed his truck. "I pay to keep my hummer here so when I travel home she's always waiting for daddy. Are you ladies ready to roll?" he smiled.

Janitta playfully hit Davion's arm. "I so hate you right now, Davion. I've wanted to buy a hummer for a few years now but I never made the time to really look into it. If it's up to my standards, I'll be buying one as soon as we get home," she said jumping inside rubbing the leather seats.

Carrie smiled. "You got it like that, Janitta money bags Delray."

"Don't get it mistaken, Ms. Carrie Baby," Janitta sang. "I know how to handle my finances."

Davion and the girls enjoyed a quick joyride around town until they reached the solemn house of their destination. He reached from behind his two companions to ring the doorbell. "Who's there?" Mrs. Hewitt called out.

"It's us, Mom," Carrie replied.

"I didn't know you were bringing my girls." she smiled.

"Oh, it's like that, Mom. I don't get a hug. You forgot about your only son now that these two brats are here."

"You know I love you, boy. I haven't seen my girls in a long time."

Janitta played with Mae's silver hair. "Hi, Mom. I've missed you. How have you been?" she asked.

"I've been blessed. Do you have any children? Are you married? Tell me what's been going on with you girls. Ever since Davion and Carrie have been calling themselves broken up you girls broke up with me," she replied.

"No children and no husband, Mrs. Mae and you know I will always love you no matter what those two crazy people do."

"I know you will. That makes my dear old heart happy. Now, about the babies. What are you waiting on?"

"A good man," Janitta joked.

"Mom, where is Felicia?" Davion walked into the den.

"She's upstairs in her room. She hasn't come out in days."

Davion headed upstairs. "Well, ladies, it sounds like we have a lot of work on our hands." Carrie and Janitta followed Davion to the room Felicia vowed to never depart. Davion eased the door open. "How are you doing baby sis?"

"How do you think I feel? I lost my baby."

"I'm sorry, that was a dumb question. I have some very special people here to see you."

Felicia tried to focus her teary eyes. "Oh, hi Carrie, I haven't talked to you in such a long time. Who is that behind you?"

"It's me," Janitta jumped out with her arms open.

"Where the heck have you been stranger?" Felicia managed to smile.

"I've been around. I'm sorry to hear about the baby."

"Thank you for caring. Why are you being so quiet, Davion?"

"I don't want to put my foot in my mouth again. Where's your hubby?" Davion asked.

"Who knows, ask mom. I haven't seen him today."

"I think I'd be better off with Robert and leave you ladies to it." Davion escaped to find his brother-in-law.

"Bye, punk," Felicia yelled.

Janitta opened the blinds to let the light shine into the gloomy room. "What do you plan on doing? Are you going to stay in this bed forever?"

"Maybe I will." Felicia covered her head with the multi-colored blanket.

"No, you're not. You're going to get out of this bed." Janitta moved closer to the bed.

"I know I should, but I can't bring myself to it." Felicia pounded the pillow into her head.

"Yes, you can and you will. Now, get out of this bed." Janitta pulled the blanket off the bed.

"Don't you get it, Janitta? I lost my baby. I gave birth to my baby that was dead before she came into this world. Could you imagine that?"

"We could never put ourselves in your shoes. We've never experienced what you're going through. Life is full of ups and downs, but it's up to us to find a way to keep moving forward. You have so many people around you who love you. Your brother doesn't know what to say and I can't imagine how your husband is feeling." Carrie paced the room.

"I don't know how Robert feels, either, because he won't hang around long enough for me to find out."

Janitta pulled the blanket completely off the bed. "Well, we won't stick around either if you don't get up. Give me your hand and get up. Be strong."

"I haven't seen you in years and you're just going to come in here and start bossing me around."

"That's right. Now get your funky behind up." Janitta hit Felicia's leg.

"Okay, okay. I'll get up and take a shower."

"That sounds like a plan. We'll get your clothes ready and you go get you all dolled up so you can get out of the house for a while," Janitta said.

Carrie hurried to call Davion. "Hey, we convinced Felicia to get out of bed so we're going to hang out for a while tonight."

"How did you manage to do that?" Davion asked.

"We got skills," she sang and turned to go back upstairs.

The three women took turns showering in the small bathroom and dressed in their sexiest outfits for a night out on the town. They left soon after. "It's been a long time since we all went out together." Felicia smeared her body butter on her toned legs.

"I think the last time we went out, we were all packed in Davion's black Infiniti," Carrie reminisced.

Janitta laughed. "Oh, man, I remember the Infiniti. He was nuts about that car. He used to talk crazy to anyone who touched it."

"How long are you going to smear that body butter all over you Mrs. Felicia?" Carried laughed.

"As long as I need woman. I don't want to be the ashy girl in the club."

Janitta laughed. "Oh, I guess you want to avoid what happened to you the night you wore your little black dress."

Felicia hit Janitta's arm. "Shut the heck up Janitta. Some things are better left in the past."

Carrie held her stomach in laughter. "No, no, Janitta. You have to tell the story. You have to tell it now."

Janitta looked at Felicia. "Forgive me sis but I can't disappoint my audience. You were dancing so hard that night, I guess you were sweating a lot. Girl, after we left the club to hit up the diner and you bent over to sit down and that dress rose up," Janitta could barely get the words out in between the laughter. "Your dang legs from the thighs up were ashy as hell."

Felicia covered her face with her hands. "Oh my gosh. I can't believe you are doing this to me. I thought we vowed to never talk about that again."

"I know, I'm sorry but seeing you with all that body lotion," she took a deep breath. "I had to do it."

"Oh my gosh, that was the most embarrassing night of my life. Ever since that happened, whenever I go out I have to make sure my skin is thoroughly hydrated." Felicia cringed thinking of that night.

Carrie grabbed her purse. "Where are your car keys Felicia?"

"They should be downstairs on the table by the front door." She slid her heels on.

"I'll meet you guys downstairs. Janitta, you are too much and that's why I love your behind." Carrie ran downstairs.

Janitta snatched the lotion away from Felicia. "Dang girl, you don't have to look like you're about to be fried. That's enough. Let's get out of here. You know how impatient Carrie can get."

Felicia jumped from the chair. "Gosh Janitta, take a breath. I forgot how much you talk." The ladies ran downstairs to the garage to see Carrie already had the car revved up and ready to go.

"I was wondering what was taking you so long."

Janitta and Felicia looked at each other and burst into laughter. "I told you," Janitta said.

Carrie backed out of the garage and sped down the street. "You told her what?"

"How impatient you get."

Carrie stopped at the red light. "I beg to differ. I'm not the impatient one in this group."

"Yeah right. You're the worst." Janitta pointed at a group of men in a truck who also appeared to be headed out for a night on the town. "Ladies, look to your right and look to your left. We have fine Montana men everywhere."

Carrie sang. "Felicia, I know you have to be feeling this." She entered the highway.

"Yeah, you're right. I needed this. You two better watch me tonight because my husband hasn't been showing me any attention and I don't know what kind of trouble I may get into. Oh, hey Carrie go to that club right there. I love this club."

"You better be good," Janitta replied.

"Looks like the one we need to watch is Miss Thing over here putting all this shiny mess on her lips."

"Oh, don't hate me because I'm beautiful."

Felicia placed her hand over her chest. "So what are you saying. Janitta and I are your ugly friends."

Janitta opened the door as soon as Carrie turned the ignition off. "Speak for yourself. I'm all that and then some."

The ladies stepped out the car all tugging on their clothes to make quick adjustments. "I know everyone here, so we won't need to wait in line or pay." Felicia said.

"Oh, you got it like that," Janitta replied.

"Of course, that's why I know I'm the pretty girl in this crew," Felicia dusted her shoulder off.

"Okay, okay, I see you." The ladies were greeted by the bouncer as they walked into the club.

They immediately gravitated toward the dance floor. Felicia closed her eyes as she swayed and moved to the music. "What are you guys doing here?" Davion crept up on the dancing women.

"Same thing you're doing, but by the looks of it, better." Felicia joked.

Carrie laughed. "You never had rhythm. I can't remember how long I've tried to teach you how to dance."

It didn't take Davion long to make his way over to Carrie. He wrapped his arms around her waist and they rocked side to side to Keri Hilson's song, *Slow Dance*. "You smell so good, baby." He kissed her neck.

"Thank you. This night is going to be branded in my memory. It's been so long since we've enjoyed each other like this."

"I know you just got here but how about we blow this place and get some alone time." Davion said.

"Umm, let me tell the girls," Carrie replied.

"Wait, you don't want to think about it?"

"Heck no, I was hoping you would ask me that," Carrie replied.

"Sounds like a plan. I'll meet you out front, sexy."

Carrie disappeared in the crowd while Davion recovered his car from the valet.

***

Davion and Carrie woke in each other's arms that morning. Carrie was his drug and he needed his fix. "How did you sleep?" He stared into her eyes.

"Like a baby. What time is it? Why are you up so early sweetie?" Carrie asked.

"I have something on my mind I need to ask you about."

"What is it?" Carrie sat up in the cozy bed.

"Do you still have the same love for me as you had when we were engaged living together?"

"I'll always love you. I long for your touch. Terrence is my husband and even he can't satisfy me the way you do. Call me crazy, but you're forever going to be in my heart, baby. You have always been there for me. Anytime I needed someone to confide in, you were there. When I went through my heart problems, you were there. Davion, I can't remember a time when you weren't there for me. However, I have to think about the well-being of my daughter."

"I need to tell you something." He took a deep breath.

"Oh no, this must be bad because you just put your serious face on early in the morning," she laughed.

"Be serious baby. Do you know Cynthia McRynalds?" Davion asked.

"Yes, she's Terrence's ex-girlfriend."

"Before I got the call about my sister, she came to my office. She gave me the whole spill as to why she needed a lawyer. Of course, I couldn't take her case because of you. She's Terrence's ex-wife. She's pregnant and she's been fighting for her spousal and child support for quite some time now."

"What do you mean his *ex-wife*? He told me they just dated and what do you mean she's pregnant? " Carrie stood and paced the floor.

"You didn't know they were once married?"

"Hell no, he never told me they were married. All he ever says is they dated. I can't believe this. I feel like a dang fool."

"You shouldn't feel that way, baby. You're a wonderful woman. How could you know?"

"Well, for starters his family could have clued me in on the dang details. I need to go home. He probably has Cynthia in my house as we speak."

"I would hope he would have more sense than to bring her into your marital bed."

"I knew he was lying but I didn't want to believe it. I feel all I ever do is cry over something Terrence is doing or has been putting me through lately. I can't take anymore."

"A man never realizes what he has in a woman until he loses her. I can take the blame for what I did, but this is not your fault and I'm not saying this just because I love you."

"I really don't have anything positive to say in favor of men right now."

Davion wiped her tears away. "Carrie, if you give me a chance I want to be a better friend to you and eventually be a better man for you."

Carrie rested her head on Davion's bulky chest. "I'm sorry for not giving us chance. Terrence has hit me with too much for me to continue with him. I don't know who he is and I feel like everything he's ever told me has been a lie. Don't laugh at me but I have been thinking about you a lot. I was wondering if we were to take things slow… how would you feel about us getting back things back together. But, first I need to ask Terrence to leave my house and I want you by my side when I tell him. I don't know how he'll react."

"There's no doubt about me wanting to the man in your life. However, are you sure you want to be there when you discuss something so personal with your husband?" Davion asked.

"I've never been so sure about anything in my life."

"Okay, well, since I know Felicia will be okay I guess we can check on a flight to head back home as soon as possible."

Carrie buried her face in her hands. "I cannot believe this is happening to me. Every time I think I get love right. I find out I'm completely wrong again. I don't know what else I can do?"

Davion brushed her hair away from her face. "Please don't fault yourself for what he's doing. You're not the one to blame. Lie back and close your eyes. I'll find us a flight home." He kissed the back of her neck.

Carrie rested her head in Davion's lap and texted her plans of going home to Janitta. "Thank you sweetie. I knew Terrence and I were moving too fast. Had I took more time and not been so blinded comparing him to you, I wouldn't be going through all of this."

Davion jotted details on a notepad. "One second, let me book this flight."

"Oh no, I'm just thinking out loud. I know you're handling business." She tapped her legs and stared at the ceiling.

"Okay, thank you." Davion ended his call. "Baby, stop blaming yourself and please don't fall into any type of depression. You're better than that. I booked us on a six o'clock flight today."

"Great." Carrie rose from the bed.

"Come on crazy lady and let's go get the double duo and go to breakfast." He patted her bottom.

"Sounds like a plan." She kissed her beau's neck.

Chapter Ten

Finally the three made it back to Los Angeles and dropped Janitta off at home and headed to Carrie's house. "I'm going to ask you one more time before we walk in your house and change your life as you know it. Are you sure you want to do this with me in there?" Davion asked.

"Very," Carrie replied grabbing his hand.

"Wow, I know what this means."

"What are you talking about?"

"For as long as I've known you, anytime you answer with one word, you're steaming mad."

"I want answers and I need a resolution." They looked at each other and proceeded to go inside the house.

Terrence walked down the stairs. "What the hell is he doing here?" he pointed at Davion.

"Don't worry about Davion. I need to talk to you." Carrie waved her hand.

"Fuck that, answer my question Carrie."

"If you let me talk, you'll understand why Davion's here."

"Then talk," Terrence urged.

"I know you were still seeing Cynthia. What I don't understand is why you never told me you two were married." Carrie paced the floor talking waving her hands erratically.

"I was never married before you. What the heck are you talking about," Terrence asked.

"This will go a heck of a lot smoother if you just tell me the truth. Regardless of the matter you will not be in this house after tonight." Carrie pointed to the door.

"You know this is not the way you need to handle any issue you have with me. We need to talk about this alone. This doesn't have anything to do with Davion." Terrence pleaded.

Davion moved closer. "I'm here to make sure you show Carrie the respect she deserves. I won't give my opinion on anything between the two of you."

"I should be beating your ass for sleeping with my wife. Yeah, I know what you two have been up to." Terrence pounded his fist into his hand.

"I want to see you beat my ass. I'll be the last man you try that on." Davion stood face-to-face with Terrence.

"You think so, little man." Terrence laughed.

Carrie stepped between the two heated men. "Let's not get off the subject. What you have done is far beyond repairable and I want you to leave my house now."

"Leave, hell no. Half of this is mine." Terrence held his arms out.

"You really believe you can come into my house that I owned long before there was a you and I, and try to claim it? You must be out of your damn mind," Carrie laughed.

"I love you and I'm not stepping aside because you want to shack up with this idiot again."

"You're lucky I'm a bit more reserved than most women because that comment would have gotten your ass cut. Get the hell out," she screamed.

"I never thought I would say this but you're a coldhearted bitch. I don't know what your problem is but you need to fix it. Our vows were till death do us part. I went the extra mile for you because I knew your worth. This guy didn't even have the balls or common sense to wife you and yet you're defending him like he walks on water."

"This marriage is dead. Now please leave." Carrie pointed to the door.

"So, how far are you going with this because you can't take my daughter away from me Carrie?"

"We can make arrangements about Taysha later, or you could just sign over your parental rights."

"I love my daughter and I'm not giving her up. Could we talk alone for a second, please Carrie?"

"Sure, I'm willing to do whatever it takes for you to leave."

Terrence led her into the other room. "Are you thinking about moving Davion in here with my daughter? Don't you think she's been through enough changes?" Terrence asked.

"I haven't discussed living arrangements with anyone. I just don't want to be here with you anymore." Carrie stepped back from Terrence.

"Carrie, I want you to listen to me please. I don't care if you want to leave me but you have to know. Cynthia is very smart, but she's even more conniving. I was never married to that woman and if she's pregnant. It's not by me. I can assure you of that."

"I don't think we could ever recover from all these things that keep popping up around you. Even if you aren't seeing her or weren't married to and yet she's saying these things it's better for me to exclude myself from the drama. I have to think about my daughter. We've been at each other's throats for a long time now. I'm tired of arguing with you. I'm tired of the phone calls late at night and, most of all, I'm tired of all the games."

"The only way Cynthia would even think about going to Davion with these allegations is if she has been watching you. You play a role in this too. If you weren't sleeping with Davion she wouldn't know about him. Why would you let someone else turn you against your husband?"

Davion stormed into the room. "I've heard my name come out your mouth one too many times. Discussing your marriage should not cause you to say my name that many times."

"What's your problem little man? You gave Carrie up. You walked away and now that you see her with someone else you can't stand it. Before you came back into her life, everything between the two of us was fine. What are you trying to gain with all this?" Terrence yelled.

Davion took a step back. "You need to back the hell up before you piss me off. Keep your distance. All I'm doing is hipping Carrie on the truth about her so-called marriage. Yes, I fucked up, but that doesn't mean I have to sit back and watch someone hurt her again. She's special to me and if I know someone's treating her like a second hand woman, you better believe I'm going to rectify the situation."

"Well, you can step aside, lover boy, because this is between me and my wife. Key words, Davion. She's *my wife*." Terrence pointed his finger. "Carrie, is this what you want? You want me out of your life?"

"I want you to leave. We can discuss Taysha with our lawyers."

"I'll go for now and when you cool down I'd like to talk to you alone." Terrence looked at Davion.

"She's not going to be alone with you anymore. You may as well get used to that," Davion interjected.

"Don't you ever tell me what I can and can't do like I'm some sucker." Terrence pushed his chest into Davion's chest.

"Back the hell off." Davion placed his hand on Terrence arm.

"I should have known you were nuts when I found out Ronald was your friend." Carrie rubbed her temples in a relaxing motion.

"Don't compare me to Ronald." Terrence rushed over to Carrie.

"You're acting just like him."

"So, this is what you want. You're just going to stand in here with Davion and gang up on me."

"I don't see it working any other way."

"Damn, Carrie, are things this bad in our marriage?" Terrence asked.

"We're not getting anywhere going over the same things and making no resolutions."

"So basically we can't talk because your boyfriend is here," Terrence said.

"I didn't want to embarrass you, but since you insist. You haven't been a husband or lover to me in a long time. You don't stimulate me intellectually, sexually, or emotionally. You have subjected our daughter to an atmosphere of arguing, screaming, and yelling. If I don't take a stand now and show her this is not how a man treats his wife, she will accept anything."

"Are you in love with Davion?" Terrence asked.

"I've always loved Davion. He was my first love so he'll always be in my heart."

"I'm not talking about your damn first love. I'm asking you, are you in love him Davion? Have you forgotten about me? I don't mean shit to you. You never cared about me."

"I love you and I never wanted this to happen to us. What you and I share has never compared to the love I carry in my heart for Davion. He's always shown me the utmost respect." She held Davion's hand.

"Do you hear yourself? This man left you for an entire year and never called you to even check if you were still among the living. I came along and I've been here for you. I took a bullet for you. I lost my family because of you. Ronald wouldn't have ever done what he did had I not been with you."

"How dare you stand there and blame me for everything Ronald did. He was a sick man and I'm hurt that you would even say that to me. I loved Rolonda and

Christopher and keep in mind my child was one of the people he hurt," Carrie cried.

Davion wrapped his arms around Carrie's waist. "Don't you think you've hurt her enough man?"

"I've done way too much for you to stand here and allow Davion to talk to me this way." Terrence looked into Carries eyes.

"I don't want to have to ask you to leave again," Davion said.

"Dude, you don't have anything to do with this. You need to back off," Terrence yelled.

"Don't talk to Davion like that. At least someone's looking out for me." Carrie placed her hand on Davion's back.

"His looking out for you is getting in my way. I'll be back in a couple days to get my things." Terrence disappeared into the cold night air.

Davion locked the door behind Terrence. "I don't want to be rude because I know you're feeling a lot of mixed emotions right now. But, I need to know where we stand."

Carrie sat on the staircase. "I didn't think this would be so emotionally draining. I love you, Davion. When we broke up, I didn't know how I would make it without you. I have been trying so hard to get over you that I've been doing some really messed up stuff. Dating guys because there was something about them that reminded me of you. Like it would make any difference that you were gone. I haven't been thinking clearly. All I ever wanted was a solid relationship like my mom and dad. You know firsthand what type of household I was raised in. It seems like I'll never have that life."

"Carrie, the man you're looking for is standing right before you. I know this is going to be very hard for you to deal with. I'm afraid that you'll become damaged and you'll eventually decide to let me go. I couldn't handle that."

"You mean the world to me and I'll never turn my back on you. I love you, Davion. I just need some time to process things in my head and most of all, my heart."

"Do you feel safe staying here alone tonight?" Davion asked.

"I think I'll be okay, sweetheart." She kissed Davion.

He walked toward the door. "Call me if you need me. I don't care what time. I'm here for you."

"I will." Carrie smiled.

"I'll be back first thing in the morning." He kissed her forehead.

"Here, take this key with you. I'm going to get some sleep. Thank you for being here for me like always. I really appreciate you." Carrie said showing Davion out and locking the door to sleep the night away.

Chapter Eleven

Carrie had a restless night thinking about everything that happened. She slipped on a pair of baggy sweatpants and an oversized sweatshirt and decided to grab a cup of coffee before she took her shower. Carrie smiled because she knew Davion would be over soon. But, her smile was quickly wiped away when she saw Cynthia standing inside her house. "What are you doing in here?" she asked.

Cynthia took a silver gun out of her purse. "I thought if I told you how I felt, you would see how much I love Terrence, but you still didn't see that."

Carrie held her hands up. "D-don't do this," she stammered, backing away from Cynthia.

Cynthia waved the gun as she spoke. "You're the reason why things never worked out. I never could really understand why Terrence wouldn't work things out with me, but now I do. I need you out of the way. You had a baby with my husband. You took him away from me." She shot Carrie in the stomach and ran away from the house.

Carrie held her stomach as she fell to the floor. She struggled to crawl on her knees to reach the phone, but kept sliding on the pool blood draining from her body.

Refusing to ever break another promise, Davion arrived as planned and just in time. "Carrie," he cried out. Carefully walking, Davion followed a smeared blood trail from the front door toward the office. "Carrie, what the heck happened?" he screamed, noticing Carrie on the floor gasping and fighting for every breath she took. He ran to Carrie's side as she lay on her back. "Carrie, hang on, I'm going to get help." He checked her pulse and called for help. "I need an ambulance at 1221 North Conrad Avenue. Please, my girlfriend has been shot."

***

Davion finally arrived at the hospital after he talked to the detective. "Excuse me, could I go back to see my girlfriend?" Davion asked a nurse.

"Sir, her doctor was on his out to speak with you. She has two of the best doctor's in our facility working on her. He can only speak with you for a moment."

"Thank you," Davion replied.

The doctor opened the door, and motioned for Davion to follow him to a small office. "I'd like to talk to you about Mrs. Coleman's condition."

"How is she doing?" Davion asked.

"As you know, she was shot in her stomach. The bullet has caused severe internal bleeding. She has damaged tissue and she'll need surgery. We will do our level best to stop the bleeding. If not, she could hemorrhage, which would be fatal."

"I'm sorry, doctor, I don't know what hemorrhage means."

"It means she could bleed to death. Even if we're successful in repairing the damage the bullet has caused, she will still need a blood transfusion. If we're unsuccessful with the surgery, she could die."

Davion leaned forward to catch his breath. "What are her chances for survival?"

"It's too soon to say without knowing how bad the damages are. Give us a chance to see what we're facing, and we'll let you know where things stand. I really need to

get back in there. The team is prepping her for the surgery."
He stood.

"Thank you." Davion replied. He dialed the phone
number to reach Carrie's parents.

"Hello," Maurine answered.

"Mrs. Johnson, is that you?" Davion asked.

"Yes, who's calling?"

He hesitated, "Hi, Mrs. Johnson, this is Davion. How
are you doing?"

"Oh, I can't complain baby. I haven't heard from you in
quite some time. To what do I owe the pleasure of this call
baby?" She perked up.

"I was calling because I need you to come to L.A. as
soon as possible," Davion replied.

"You sound like you've been crying. What is it baby?"
Maurine asked.

"It's very important that you come as soon as possible.
I don't want to talk about it over the phone. This is
something I must do in person. It's about Carrie. She's in
the hospital and she needs you here as soon as possible."

"Davion, just tell me what's going on."

"I promise I'll explain everything when you get here."

"Oh, my sweet baby. I'm hanging up. I need to get a
flight out, good bye."

"Call my cell when you arrive. I'll give you all the
details as soon as you get here." He gave her his phone
number.

"I'll be calling you as soon as I get there. You need to
be ready to explain everything to me and don't you dare
leave a detail out."

"I will Mrs. Johnson." Davion took a deep breath to
make his next call.

"Janitta speaking," she answered.

"Hey J, I need you to come to the Hollywood
Community Hospital right away."

"Why, What's going on?" she asked,

"Carrie's in the hospital. I need you to come as soon as you can. I need you J." Davion wiped the continuous flow of tears from his eyes.

"Of course, I'm on my way but tell me is it life threatening?" Janitta asked.

"I'd rather not talk about it over the phone. Come as soon as possible. I'll wait for you downstairs by the emergency side."

***

Janitta ran to her car. Swerving in and out of the busy lanes on the intersection, She arrived at the hospital parking in the first available spot and ran into the emergency entrance. "Davion, Davion."

"Janitta, please, sit down. I went to see Carrie this morning and when I got to her house the door was wide open. So, I walked in. I found her laying on the floor in her office damn near dead. I could tell she was shot in hall by the foyer cause there was a trail of blood like she tried to drag herself to the phone. I've only talked to the doctor once and he couldn't tell me if she would make it or not. She's in surgery, so we need to go upstairs to the waiting room in case someone comes out to talk to us." Davion took a deep breath.

"I can't even freaking think right now. This can't be real. Carrie's never had one damn enemy in her life. Who would do something like this to her?" Janitta stepped in the elevator with Davion.

Davion pushed the button to their destination. "I have a hunch. Carrie hasn't been able to talk. The police are on it and I've already told them what happened last night."

"Why don't I know shit? What are you talking about? What happened last night?" Janitta asked.

"Carrie told Terrence she wanted to end their marriage. I didn't think Terrence would take things this far."

Janitta placed her hand over her forehead. "Hold on. Why would she do that?"

"She found out some things and decided it was best for Terrence to leave."

"I can't freaking think. Oh my goodness. I need to know how she's doing."

"She's in surgery. The doctors are trying to stop the bleeding, but if they don't"—he swallowed—"she could die."

"That's not going to happen. Carrie's a strong woman. She'll get through this. She has to get through this. She's my sister, she has to get through it." Janitta placed her head into her hands praying.

"I don't know how long she was lying there. I can't believe this is happening. I can't imagine living my life without her."

"I can't lose her. I won't lose her. Everything has to be okay. It has to be. Where in the hell are the nurses? Where are the doctors? We need to know how she's doing. They can't keep us waiting like this."

"I spoke with the doctor about a half hour ago. That was the last time anyone has been out."

Janitta took a deep breath. She and Davion sat in silence for hours but those hours felt like an eternity until a tall doctor approached them. He removed his green surgical cap. "Mr. Hewitt, I have good news. We were able to control Mrs. Coleman's bleeding. Right now she's stable and we're waiting to get her blood type for her transfusion. She's not in any condition to have visitors right now, but things are looking really good."

"Thank you, Doctor." Davion smiled.

Janitta embraced Davion. "I knew everything would be fine."

He dug into his pocket to answer his vibrating cell phone.

Maurine belted into the phone. "We're here. Where do we need to go?"

"You guys must have taken a red eye. That was extremely fast. Catch a cab and come to the Hollywood Community Hospital on De Longpre Avenue."

"We'll be there shortly and you better be ready to tell me everything."

"Yes, Mrs. Johnson."

Janitta patted his back. "You know, before I got the call about Carrie, I was sitting at home contemplating taking William back. But after I got your call and prayed the entire drive over here. I realized life was too short. I need to enjoy my life. I don't want to be unhappy and settling for someone who clearly doesn't love me."

Davion smiled. "I'm happy to hear that. You're an amazing woman and you deserve an exceptional man."

"We just need to get our girl back. I have faith that things will work out for the best."

Maurine ran through the busy hospital holding Taysha with Stephanie also racing beside side her. "What floor should we go to?" she asked Davion.

"Third floor. I'll wait for you by the elevators."

"We're on our way up right now," She pushed the button to get an elevator up.

Davion and Janitta waited outside the elevator for them to arrive.

"What is going on baby? Where's my daughter?" Maurine and Stephanie were visibly out of breath.

Janitta took Taysha's hand to maintain what little innocence she had left and walked away with her until the grownups finished talking.

"This morning I went over to Carrie's house and when I got there I found her lying on the floor in a pool of blood. Someone shot her in her stomach and left her there for dead. Mrs. Johnson, she had to have emergency surgery because they needed to stop her from bleeding out. They were successful with the surgery and now she's getting a blood transfusion to replace all the blood she lost. That's what we are waiting on." He sat beside Maurine.

"Oh, my God. I want to speak to the doctor right now."

"I'll find a nurse and see if we can get him out right away."

"You do that," Maurine replied crying into her handkerchief. Janitta walked around the corner and placed her arm around Maurine.

"Calm down, Mom, everything's going to be okay. Where the hell is Terrence?" Stephanie asked, turning toward Janitta.

"Davion told me Carrie threw him out last night. I can't say he did this, but I have a strong feeling he had something to do with it. I mean, where is he now?"

"What are the police doing about this?" Stephanie asked.

Janitta shrugged her shoulders. "I don't know what's going. I just found out she threw Terrence out. Davion knows more than I do lately."

"Jesus, my baby girl," Maurine moaned retrieving a large worn Bible from her purse and holding it to her chest.

Davion walked into the waiting room with Carrie's doctor. "Hello, are you Mrs. Coleman's mother?" he asked.

"Yes, I am." She moved to the edge of her seat.

"Your daughter is a fighter. We were successful in stopping the bleeding and everything looks great for now. She's lost a lot of blood, so she we're just waiting for her blood type to do her transfusion. We should get it within the hour. She's not able to respond, but if you'd like to see her, I can allow two people in at a time."

"Before you go, Doctor, I have more questions."

"No problem, go right ahead."

"Well, I have several questions. I need to know if she'll need more surgery after today. Does she have other damages to her organs? Will she have any long-term problems beyond her need for a blood transfusion?" Maurine asked.

"She shouldn't need any more surgery and there weren't any damages to her major organs. She'll need a lot of therapy so she can improve her walking, and her digestive system will need to be monitored. Beyond these immediate concerns she should live a normal life."

"Thank you, Doctor. Could you please take me to my baby now," Maurine asked standing up.

"Yes, of course, but only two at a time."

Davion motioned. "Go ahead, Stephanie. Janitta and I can go after you two."

Maurine smiled. "Thank you, Davion."

Janitta blew out a huge breath of air that she'd been holding since Mrs. Johnson arrived. "You handled that well, Davion. I'm proud of you. What a way to man up." She patted his back.

"Thank you, Janitta." He sat down and placed his head into his hands with his elbows propped on his knees.

Janitta continued, "I haven't prayed this much in a long time. I can't remember ever being this afraid before."

"Mr. Davion, can I go see my mommy too?" Taysha asked.

"I'll have to ask your grandmother if she thinks that's a good idea when she gets back." he replied.

"I'm scared. Where is my daddy?" she questioned.

"I don't know, Taysha but I hope to know soon."

"Everything will be okay. Just be a big girl for us, okay?" Janitta said.

"I will," Taysha replied holding her head down.

"Aww, baby girl, don't be upset. If I knew where your dad was I would bring him here myself for you. Come here," Janitta replied holding her arms open to embrace the worried child.

Maurine walked into the waiting room dabbing her red eyes with her yellow handkerchief. "My baby, my baby," she sobbed.

"Granny, can I see my mommy now?" Taysha ran to Maurine.

"Mommy is very sick. Maybe in a couple of days, Taysha. Davion and Janitta you both can go on back."

She moped. "Yes, Granny. Mr. Davion, could you kiss my mommy for me?" She sat in an empty seat away from everyone.

"I sure will. Janitta, are you coming?" Davion asked.

Janitta followed Davion to a dark, impersonal hospital room. Janitta quickly went to Carrie's side and held her limp hand. "Hey, Carrie, I'm so sorry you're having to go through this but I know you'll be back to yourself in no time."

Davion wiped tears from his eyes. "I'm sorry I wasn't there to protect you. I know it's going to take some time for you to get better, but I promise I'll be by your side every step of the way. I love you so much, Carebear."

Janitta chimed in, "I love you, too. I'm here for you. Anything you need, I'm here for you."

Davion placed kisses on Carrie's cheek. "Our time is up, but I don't want to leave you, baby. You have my word. I'll be with you every step of the way. You're going to be okay, baby. I love you so much."

Carrie struggled to speak. "Cynthia."

"Janitta, did you hear that? It sounded like she said Cynthia, Is that who did this to you?" Davion asked.

Carrie closed her eyes and drifted back into a deep slumber. "I think that's what she said Davion. Who the heck is Cynthia? She's never told me anything about a Cynthia."

"It's a long story but I can't tell you about it if Carrie hasn't. That's her personal business. I can't believe this crap. I need her to talk." Davion leaned into the wall.

The nurse rubbed his arm. "Sir, be patient. She'll come around and soon you'll understand what she's saying."

"Janitta, go be with the family. I'm going to make a call to the detective and see if they can get someone here to monitor her room until Cynthia and Terrence are located."

"Okay, I will." She walked in the opposite direction back to the waiting room.

Chapter Twelve

Stephanie stood and stretched. "Mom, I'm going outside. I think I'll give Dad a call and see how he's doing with Cruella."

"Don't talk about your Aunt Jackie like that," Maurine replied. "Well, Taysha, it's just you and your old Granny. I'm sure you will be able to see your mommy really soon."

"I want to give her a big hug." Taysha jumped.

"How big of a hug do you want to give your mommy?" Maurine leaned forward.

"This big," Taysha said holding her arms out wide.

Maurine laughed at her quirky granddaughter. Stephanie walked into the waiting room. "Mom, Dad wants to talk to you." She passed the cell phone to Maurine.

"Hi, honey, how are you?" Maurine answered the phone.

"Why didn't you tell me what was going on with Carrie? I should be there," Jimmie replied.

"Sweetheart, I didn't know all the details. I didn't want to stress you out without knowing what was going on."

"Did you really need to leave me here with your sister like I'm a child who needs supervision?" Jimmie replied.

"I didn't think you should be alone with you just having a stroke. I'll be home soon enough. Just try to deal with it the best you can sweetheart."

"What do you mean I'm not in any condition to be alone? It's been six months since my last stroke. I don't care about my condition. I'll be there as soon as I can get a flight out." Jimmie huffed.

"That was your second stroke. I couldn't leave you alone and I'm not in the mood to argue with you. Put Jackie on the phone and we'll make the arrangements to get you here," Maurine replied.

Jimmie held the phone out for Jackie. "Hey, sis. How's our girl doing?" Jackie asked.

"She's a fighter."

"Well, I've been praying for her."

"I know you have, sister. I need you to do me a favor." Maurine walked with the cell phone until she reached an unoccupied area.

"Anything you need." Jackie graciously replied.

"I need you to get Jimmie a flight here. He's insisting on being with Carrie and you know how he gets when he has his mind set."

Jackie protested. "Do you think that's a good idea? He may not be able to handle heavy traveling right now."

"He doesn't have to fly the plane, Jackie. Would you just do as I asked?"

"I don't think it's a good idea. That's a pretty long flight," Jackie said.

"Jimmie was right. He should be here with us. Will you do this for me?"

"I'll call the airline now."

"Thank you, Jackie. Don't worry about making plans for his return. He'll be staying until Carrie's released."

"I'll call you with the date and time of his flight." Jackie ended the call.

***

Jackie sat the phone on the table. "Jimmie, are you sure you can handle a long flight to L.A. That's a four hour flight, you know?"

Jimmie nodded. "I need to be there for my daughter. How do you think Carrie would feel if she woke up and I was the only one missing in action?" he said.

"I get all that but how long do you plan on staying in L.A.?" Jackie asked.

Jimmie replied walking into the other room to pack his clothes, "I know where you're going with this. We've been doing this for too long. I'm going to tell you like I told you before. We're getting too old to keep playing these childish games."

Jackie followed Jimmie, swinging her hands in the air. "Where is all that coming from? I thought you and I were okay. We've been doing this for over thirty years and now you want to end it. I haven't had a serious relationship with a man because every time I try to move on I have to hear your questions about what we're doing, and if I loved him more than I love you. I've been praying for years to hear you say you're going to leave Maurine and be with me. I never realized I've been allowing my life to slip away by running after you." She touched Jimmie's shoulder.

Jimmie continued packing. "I love Maurine and I owe the world to her. Maurine's the only woman I've ever really loved. She's the one for me, not you. I've been dealing with this sickness because I was trying to juggle two women at the same time. I can't do this anymore. It's over. I need to be a better husband." The two walked down the hallway into the living room.

"How can you say you never loved me?" Jackie asked.

"It's time I told you the truth Jackie. I don't love you and I never did. I was being selfish. I figured if I could keep both you and your sister I would never have to worry about being alone if either relationship failed."

Jackie sat on the sofa. "Jimmie, there's something I've never told you and I think this is the best time to tell you."

"What is it," He zipped his overnight bag.

"My daughter, Reshay. Well, she's also your daughter," Jackie confessed.

"I always knew you were a little crazy. But, I never knew you were a damn fool. You will do anything to keep me from ending this mess with you."

"Jimmie, I'm not lying. There's no way I would lie to you about my child. Maybe that's the reason I've been trying so hard to hold onto you all these years."

"Why wouldn't you ever say anything before? Hell, you better be lying." Jimmie looked in Jackie's eyes.

"I never said anything because I didn't want to be the reason my sister's fantasy life failed."

"You're evil as hell. I can't believe you would do something so damn underhanded."

"I don't need you or anyone to believe me. Reshay doesn't know you're her father and I never planned on her finding out. I just thought you should know." Jackie looked down to avoid Jimmie's judgmental stares.

"You should have told me about this when you were pregnant with her. How are we supposed to drop this bombshell on Reshay and everyone else? All she's ever known was that her father passed away years ago. How do you expect Reshay to react to this? We're going to hurt a lot of damn people with this shit Jackie." He shook Jackie by her shoulders.

"Will you please calm down, Jimmie. I'm not planning on telling anyone about this. I just thought you should know Shay is not your niece, she's your daughter."

"How in the hell could I know this and not say anything to her?" Jimmie replied.

"I have always wanted to tell her the real deal. But, every time I got the courage, I couldn't go through with it. I thought about how much I would hurt my sister and selfishly I didn't want to live without her in my life," Jackie said.

"You can't blame yourself. We've been running around not caring who we hurt or what we we're doing. Now look at all the pain we're going to cause." Jimmie rubbed his pounding head.

"I don't want to tell anyone about this. If you tell the family, it'll be your choice," Jackie replied.

"You know what kind of man I am. I could never have a child in this world and not acknowledge him or her. I know Reshay is a grown woman, but I still want her to know who she is. How could you lie to your own child all these years and not care," Jimmie asked.

"I love you and that love is why I never told Shay the truth. I always knew you loved Maurine more than you ever loved me. I knew if I told you the truth it could go one or two ways. Your marriage to Maurine could become stronger if you worked it out or you could be all mine. I wasn't willing to take the risk of pushing you two together. Hell, you should be thanking me because if I had told, you could've lost everything."

Jimmie yelled, "Why in the hell should I be thanking you? If you had told me about this a long time ago, the wounds would have healed by now for everyone. But no, you had to wait until we were old as hell to have to deal with this."

"You're the one insisting on telling everyone. Why can't you just leave it as it is and keep your mouth shut?"

"Jackie, if you're going to keep talking this reckless, you need to go." Jimmie pointed at the door.

"Why are you taking the high road on this when you've been laying with me for years?" Jackie replied.

"Because this is about a woman knowing who the hell she really is and where she comes from. I need to know if Phillip knew the truth because if you never told the man and he died believing a lie that would make you the lowest of low." Jimmie surfed through the computer to get the phone number to the airport.

"Yes, Phillip knew, but he respected my decision and he wanted a child. So, it was a win-win situation for both him and myself. Not to mention Reshay would benefit either way." Jackie shrugged her shoulders.

Jimmie shook his head. "It's a shame that I had to get this old to see the error in my ways. All I've ever done was try to keep this affair out of sight out of mind for over thirty years and now everything is about to hit the fan."

"I know the feeling."

Reshay walked in the house smiling like always. How's Carrie doing, Uncle Jimmie?" She asked taking off her pink sweater, revealing a green tank top. She loved to sport her AKA sorority colors.

"She's fine honey, have a seat. We need to talk to you." Jimmie said.

"No, I'll tell her. It's not your place." Jackie cut Jimmie off.

"Well, would one of you tell me?" Reshay demanded.

"I need to explain some things to you, baby." She smoothed her clothes.

"Mom, out with it."

"First I just want to say, I know I was wrong. But, I need to tell you who your real father is."

"Hold on, did you just say what I think you said? I know who my real father is, right. For twenty-seven years I've known that."

"Please, let me explain baby."

"You're not making any sense. Phillip is my father. He's the only father I've ever known."

Jackie took a deep breath. "Jimmie is your biological father. I couldn't tell you because, selfishly, I didn't want to become alienated by the entire family and most of all by Maurine."

"Mom, Uncle Jimmie," Reshay paced the floor, "this is a joke, right? I mean, what kind of sick game are you two playing?" Reshay put her hand to her forehead and the other on her hip.

"No, this is not a joke. Jimmie is your father," Jackie explained.

"How long have you known you were my father and all this time you never thought to be in my life as my father?"

"I could never be that kind of man. I just found out today, the same as you."

"I can't believe you didn't tell anyone mom. You have totally deprived me of knowing who my real father was and having a real relationship with Carrie and Stephanie as my sisters."

"Don't be so dramatic Reshay. You've always had a father. Phillip raised you and loved you as his own child."

"I don't know if I could ever forgive you for what you've done. What am I supposed to do? Accept old Uncle Jimmie as my father and forget about my dad?"

"No, but I do want you to eventually accept him as your father," Jackie replied.

"Is this what you want, Uncle Jimmie?" Reshay asked.

"I've never turned my back on my children. It doesn't matter the situation. I know this isn't easy to accept, but I want you to know I'm here for you. You're my child." Jimmie touched her hand.

"Mom, I need to ask you something and I need you to be honest."

"Yes, of course, anything baby."

"I get the feeling that you were never going to tell me about this. Is that true?" Reshay asked.

"I won't lie to you anymore, so no, I wasn't planning on ever telling anyone about this. Things got a little heated with Jimmie and it slipped came out."

Reshay charged toward the door. "So, the only reason you told me today is because you and old Uncle Jimmie were arguing. I don't even want to look at you right now!"

"Shay, don't leave. I want to talk about this," Jimmie said grabbing Reshay's arm.

"I can't do this, Uncle Jimmie. The only man I know and accept as my father is Phillip. I can't change the way I feel overnight. You have to give me time to process all these changes. Please respect my need for space." Reshay opened the door to leave.

"Sure, I can accept that you need your space, but I don't want you to hate your mother. She was only doing what she thought was right. I agree it was a pretty rotten decision but it was what she thought was best for everyone. Look at it this way. At least you know I've always loved you, regardless. I have always been there for you when you needed me."

"No, Reshay you can't leave. We need to talk. Jimmie, don't let her leave," Jackie replied.

"Let her go. She's trying to make sense of all this. You need to give her the space she's asking for so she can find a way to deal with this. You have to trust she will forgive you."

"Shay's all I've got," Jackie cried.

"How do you think my wife and children are going to feel about this? I may be in the same boat as you. Alone," Jimmie screamed.

"Maurine isn't going to turn her back on you. She loves you way too much to do that. She's just be upset. It will pass." Jackie waved her hand in the air.

"If you know how much Maurine loves me, then why have you continued seeing me all these years?"

"I kept seeing you because unlike you, I loved you. But, now that you've been bitten by this truth bug, I realize I was in love all by myself."

"You're a grown woman, so you know that if a man is married and never left his wife. Then you know what the deal is Jackie."

"So, what does that say about your damn character?"

"Listen, I don't have time to hear your opinions about my decisions. All you had to do was tell me Reshay was my daughter. I would've been there for her regardless of the situation. Reshay doesn't deserve this Jackie. We're all adults and we made this shit storm."

"Don't stand there and tell me what Shay doesn't deserve. You think I don't already know that? You think I don't feel like shit holding this in all these years Jimmie?

You don't know how many times I wanted to tell you but you were already treating her just like she was your daughter. I didn't want to shake things up."

"You can't be this clueless. I should have been more than just an uncle to that girl. Why can't you understand that," Jimmie asked.

"I can't understand it Jimmie because I don't want to believe I've been this selfish," Jackie cried.

"I was at fault just the same as you, if not more."

"You're just saying that to make me feel better. I was such a fool. Phil was a good man, but I shouldn't have gone along with this lie for him or for my own selfish reasons."

"I'm sure Phillip did whatever he could do to avoid losing you." Jimmie patted her back.

"Phillip was a really good man. I should've married him years before he passed but I was too busy running after you," Jackie cried and wiped her runny nose.

"Go wash your face and I'm going to keep looking for a flight out of here today."

"So, you're still going to leave after all of this? We have things we need to talk about."

"I'm not going to tell you again that I need to be with my daughter. You and Shay are welcome to come with me because it's true, we need to figure this mess out. But, I need to be where my daughter is," Jimmie replied.

"If you insist on telling everyone, I think you need to wait until Carrie is better. All of Maurine's thoughts should be with her."

Jimmie placed the phone to his ear to call the airline. "Hello is someone there?" he heard sobs in the phone.

"I heard everything. How could you do this to me you bastard?" Maurine replied.

"Maurine, what in the world are you doing on this phone?" Jimmie asked.

"Jackie didn't hang up the phone earlier. How could you lie to me about being a faithful husband for over thirty years?"

"Maurine, you don't understand what you heard. Please, let me explain," Jimmie begged.

"What more do you need to explain? You've been lying to me for years. How could you continue to say you love me, and sleep with my sister at the same time?" Maurine asked.

"Maurine, I was dead wrong for what I've done. Could you ever find it in your heart to forgive me, honey?"

"I don't deserve this after all I've done. As far as I'm concerned it's over."

"Just give me a chance to talk to you face-to-face. I know we can work this out."

"Put Jackie on the phone," Maurine demanded.

"Um, H-hello." Jackie stammered.

"How did this start?" Maurine asked.

"Are you sure this is something you want to know? Don't ask me anything you can't handle because I'm done with lying."

"I'm only going to ask you this one more time. Answer carefully. How did this affair start Jackie?" Maurine asked.

"When you introduced Jimmie to the family, shortly after that we started seeing each other off and on. In the beginning we only shared friendly conversations. Somehow it evolved into something much more than we ever planned."

"So, the entire time I've been with Jim, you have as well. How could you do this to your own sister? You were the maid of honor at my wedding."

Jackie walked into an empty room. "That was the hardest thing I've ever had to do, but I had to do that in order to keep Jimmie in my life. You don't know how badly I wanted to say something during that sham of a wedding. But, I knew if I did I would lose Jimmie. I was willing to do anything for him."

"The nerve of you to call my wedding a sham. I always knew you were loose and would do whatever with whomever but my husband. What kind of person are you?" Maurine asked.

"Do you think I'm proud of what I've done?" Jackie said.

"You don't seem to have any remorse."

Jackie whispered, "I love Jimmie and for years I've had to watch you with my man. Well, now you'll have to watch him with me sister."

"Oh, so he's you're man now. Then tell me why your man has been my husband all these years? Now, you put Jimmie back on the phone." Maurine spat into the phone.

Jackie returned by Jimmie's side. "Your turn." She passed him the phone.

"Hello," Jimmie answered.

"For over thirty years I've been a faithful and committed wife and this is how you show your appreciation. Let me tell you something. You get Jackie to help you move your stuff out of my house and you better be out when I get home."

"Maurine, listen—" Jimmie pleaded.

Maurine interrupted, "Save it. There's nothing you can say. You have no credibility as a man. Right now, you're nothing to me."

"Maurine, please don't do this. I love you with everything in me. I don't want to play games with you and I'm sorry for all the pain I've caused, but I can't let you go. I know there has to be a way for us to work this out. Thirty years is a lot of time to throw away. Hello, Maurine. Are you still there?" he asked.

"Did she hang up?" Jackie asked.

"Damn, you have the worst timing," Jimmie said, hanging up the phone.

"Yeah, I can't disagree with you on that," Jackie replied.

"I need you to call me a cab. I found a flight online and I need to go. I have a lot of work to do. I don't know how I'm going to smooth this over but I need to do something."

***

Maurine wiped the tears from her face and returned to the waiting room. "Okay, so I think we all need to go so we can get some rest while Carrie's asleep."

Davion stood. "I'd be more than happy to have everyone come over to my house. I just wouldn't feel right with you all at Carrie's house after everything that's happened."

"Please, if you don't mind. I really need to get some sleep." Maurine and Stephanie gathered their things.

Davion retrieved his keys. "I'll go get the truck and meet you all at the main entrance."

***

Stephanie squinted her eyes from the morning sunlight. "Hello," she answered the ringing phone.

"Good morning, honey, it's your dad. I need someone to pick me up at the airport."

"Dad what are you doing here? You have no business traveling in your condition." Stephanie looked at her watch.

"Well, I'm here. Now, could you please come pick me up?" Jimmie asked.

"Okay dad. We're at Davion's house and he lives really close to the airport. I'll wake him up." She stood from the bed and walked down the hall.

"Okay, I'll be waiting." Jimmie ended the call.

Stephanie announced herself as she walked into the dark bedroom. "Davion," she whispered.

"Yes," he answered.

"Could you take me to the airport to pick up my dad?" Stephanie asked.

Davion yawned. "I thought you're Dad had a stroke. Is he supposed to be traveling?"

"He did and he shouldn't be, but I guess with Carrie's condition he didn't care about his own health."

Davion quickly dressed. "You guys have a great father."

"Yeah, he's been really good to us. There isn't anything he wouldn't do." They walked down the stairs quietly to avoid waking Taysha and Maurine.

The two entered the garage. "How are Stan and the girls doing?" Davion asked backing out of the garage.

"Stan's doing really well and girls are getting bigger every day. Izzy's birthday is this month. She'll be twelve years old." Stephanie fastened her seatbelt.

"Wow, Izzy's growing up. I remember when she was a little squirmy looking thing." Davion entered the traffic to the airport.

"Well, you know we have to address the elephant in the room. Of course we are a family that tries to respect each other's space, but I have to say. I'm so happy you guys are back in each other's lives. Don't get me wrong, Terrence was a good guy in the beginning. But, I don't know what happened to make him change. One day he turned into this negative person and he's been the same negative person for a while now. I don't want him to bring my sister down any more than he already has."

"You don't have to worry about that. Terrence won't be bringing anybody down with his mess." He zoomed down the highway.

"You seem pretty sure about that. Just how close have you and Carrie gotten?" Stephanie asked.

"You'll have to talk to Carrie about that." Davion drove up to the passenger pick up area of the airport.

Stephanie pointed. "There's my dad. Hey, Daddy," she said rolling the window down.

"Hey, kiddos, it's nice to see your faces." He packed his things into the back of the SUV.

"Dad, I don't know why you don't trust us to take care of Carrie. You should be resting."

"Steph, I'm fine. I can rest here just the same as at home. Where is Maurine?" Jimmie asked.

"She's asleep. She's been a bit withdrawn since last night."

"I have an idea why. How's my baby girl holding up?" Jimmie asked.

"I believe the doctors started her blood transfusion last night. She'll be better in no time," Davion answered.

"Do the police have any idea who could have done this? Where the hell is Terrence?" Jimmie asked,

"I talked to the detective. I don't know if Terrence had anything to do with it, but I know for sure Carrie said Cynthia's name yesterday."

"Who the hell is Cynthia. Why would this person want to hurt Carrie?" Jimmie asked.

"Cynthia is Terrence's ex-wife. She has been making harassing phone calls to Carrie's house and she started popping up at both Carrie and Terrence jobs. She hasn't found it within herself to let Terrence go."

"Carrie has always been a secretive person but to not tell us something like this is beyond me," Stephanie said.

"If I had known that bastard had Carrie wrapped up in all this kind of mess I would've been here to make his ass get out," Jimmie said shaking his head.

"Dad, language," Stephanie said.

"I have to get this stuff off my chest. I'm not having this with you girls. If you want to be with someone that's fine with me but the least he could do is respect you. I don't want to ever lose either of you behind some ignorant ass man and a woman who can't let go," Jimmie babbled.

"I'm home now, so I won't let anything happen to Carrie. I give you my word."

"You need to make damn sure you stick to your word on that. You can't be pulling that disappearing act like you did before if you're going to be looking out for her. You really hurt my baby when you left," Jimmie said.

"I apologize for that. Carrie has forgiven me and I can only hope you all will do the same. I realize how stupid my decision to leave was and I won't ever let her go. Not anymore," Davion explained.

"I sure do love coming here. It's always sunny in California. You can't beat that."

"You should visit more often," Davion replied parking in the garage.

"I'm more than sure I will have more time to visit really soon," he mumbled stepping out of the truck to grab his luggage.

"Dad, let me get that for you. You can go inside with Mom." Stephanie grabbed Jimmie's luggage.

"I'm fine June bug, don't fuss over me."

"Are you sure, Dad?" Stephanie stepped back.

"Yes, honey, I'm sure."

"I'll be inside if you need me."

"Could you send your mom out, please?"

Stephanie turned to go inside the house. "She may still be asleep but I'll check for you.

"Thank you June Bug."

Stephanie ran inside. "Mom, I'm sorry to wake you but Dad's here and he wants to talk to you."

"When did he get here?" Maurine rubbed her sleepy eyes.

"We just picked him up at the airport this morning."

"Thank you, honey." Maurine rolled over in the bed.

"Well, Mom, aren't you going to go talk to Dad?" Stephanie asked.

"No, Stephanie. I'm not going outside to talk to your Dad." She covered her head with the blanket.

Stephanie looked at Davion standing behind her. "What was that all about?" She closed the door and walked down the hall.

"I have no idea and I'm not getting involved," Davion replied.

Jimmie stood in the doorway. "Davion, could you come here for a minute."

Davion looked at Stephanie and shrugged his shoulders. "What's up?" he stood outside.

"If it's okay with you, I'd like to stay at Carrie's house while I'm here."

"I don't think it's safe for you to be over there right now."

"Son, I'll be fine," Jimmie replied.

"I guess if that's what you want. We were going to see Carrie soon. Would you like to go with us first before going to her house?"

"Of course. She's the reason why I'm here," Jimmie replied.

"Well, do you think you could chill out here for a while?" Davion asked.

"I guess so." Jimmie sat on the lawn chair.

"I know I may be out of place asking you this but is everything okay?"

"No, everything's in shambles and I don't know how to fix it this time," Jimmie replied.

"Hey, Mom and Taysha are getting dressed so we can go back to the hospital. Will you two be ready to go soon?" Stephanie asked.

"Yes sweetie," Jimmie replied.

"Is everything okay out here?" Stephanie asked.

"We're ready," Maurine said holding Taysha's hand.

"Cool, let's head out. Stephanie, did you call Janitta and let her know we would be going to the hospital this morning?" Davion walked to the truck.

"I told her last night. She said she would be there." Stephanie buckled her seatbelt.

The drive to the hospital was strangely quiet. Davion rushed through the highway as quickly as possible in order to get out of the uncomfortable silence. Davion noticed Janitta sitting inside her car in the parking lot so he parked next to her.

Janitta jumped out her car with a smile as she walked around to the passenger side of Davion's truck. "Hey, you guys. I can't wait to see my girl. Mr. Johnson, how are you doing? It's really good to see you." Janitta walked with everyone to the elevator to the hospital.

"Janitta Delray, you're looking good young lady. How's life treating you?" Everyone stepped into the elevator.

"Life is really good. No complaints here," Janitta replied.

"I second that," Stephanie replied.

Maurine huffed as she exited the elevator. "Taysha, are you ready to see your mommy?" she asked.

"Yes, I am. Yes, I am. Yes, yes, yes," Taysha sang.

"Aww my precious little one. I want you to go with your Aunt Stephanie and Janitta. I'll be there in a second."

"Hey, wait for me, you guys." Davion hurried away.

"Does this mean you're ready to talk?" Jimmie asked grabbing Maurine's hand.

"Get your hands off me. You can talk without touching me you liar. I should have believed my niece Willa when she told me she saw you and Jackie running around in Ohio. She always said something was up with that."

"When did Willa tell you that? She never saw me in Ohio with Jackie," Jimmie said.

"Yes, she did see you Jimmie. I told you when you came home off the road that following week. I should have listened to her and Helen when they kept telling me not to just let it go. I feel so stupid behind you," Maurine said.

"Your sister Helen never liked me and Willa has always been tough on any man. But, I have to admit things now. I was with Jackie and yes, she did used to go with me on the road when I was driving trucks. It was always easy to do because she never came around that much. I'm sorry you had to find out about me and Jackie this way. I should have told you years ago I don't know what I was thinking," Jimmie admitted.

"Don't speak negative about my sister Helen. God rest her soul. She and Willa weren't the only people who said you were shady. My cousin Ricky has always said you weren't right. Maybe they all knew something about you that I never did. How could I be so blind?" Maurine walked in circles in the hallway.

"Good God, let's not run down the list of your family members who can't stand me. I never wanted to hurt you. I love you. I was just trying to feel more like a man when I was with both you and Jackie," he explained.

Maurine folded her arms over her chest. "Don't feed me lies. Shay is your child which means you were having unprotected sex with Jackie."

"What does that have to do with anything? I'm standing here trying to work things out with you. I was wrong, but you can't throw away thirty years just like that," Jimmie said.

"I have lost all trust in you. We can't make it without trust."

"Just give me a chance. I know I can make things better."

"Our entire marriage has been a huge lie."

"That was because of my selfish ways Maurine. Please don't give up on me. I'm begging you dear."

"You're a coward, and I don't need a coward in my life."

Jimmie looked down. "I know I am."

"I don't want to be bothered with you or Jackie while I'm here for Carrie. When we get back home, I want you to move out Jimmie."

"You can't be serious. You can't do this to us or our family."

"When did you start caring about our family?" Maurine asked.

"Would you at least act like you normally would when everyone is around? We should let everyone know when the time is right."

"You're right. I'll leave you to tell your dirty little secret to the family. I'm embarrassed enough as it stands."

"I don't mind being the one to tell everyone. When Jackie and Reshay get here later tonight, we can get everyone together."

"When were you going to tell me Jackie was bringing her snake tail into town? I told you I don't want to see that woman."

"*That woman* is your sister and she has a huge part in this as well."

"Fine, let's do it." Maurine walked away.

***

Jackie ran through her house packing everything she needed for her trip. "Shay, why don't you ever knock? You scared the living daylights out of me. I didn't expect to see you today."

"Why knock when I have a key mother. You got one over on me today when you told me old Uncle Jimmie was my father."

"Honey, please don't act this way."

"Let's talk. Didn't you want to talk?" Shay replied sitting in a nearby chair.

"I want to salvage our relationship. I know you're hurt, but you have to know I love you and I did this for you." Jackie replied.

"I don't understand how you could do this to Aunt Maurine. You know how much she loves old Uncle Jimmie."

"I wasn't thinking about Maurine. Why can't anyone see how much I love that man? Why is it all about Maurine, Maurine, Maurine?" Jackie cried.

"Listen to you. You sound like a maniac mom. Thinking about yourself. You're so selfish my well-being never even crossed your mind. "

Jackie rolled her eyes. "I knew this news would destroy lives and I wasn't ready for that."

"How long was the affair mom?" Reshay asked.

"It started long before you were born, honey." She brushed her hair.

"This is nauseating." Reshay leaned forward and held her stomach.

Jackie knelt down in front of Reshay. "I want you go to L.A. with me."

"Why are you going to L.A.? What are you up to?" Reshay asked.

"The entire family will be there and Jimmie and I have decided this would be the perfect time to lay everything out on the table."

"I can't watch you two hurt Aunt Maurine with this madness."

"There we go again with this Maurine talk. Why can't you be on my side? I'm your mother."

"Some mother you are, but I'll go under one condition," Reshay said standing.

"What would that be," Jackie asked.

"If there comes a time when I feel like I need get away. I don't want you to stop me."

"I can deal with that. I'll call the airline to get you a ticket. Now, run home and pack and I'll be by to pick you up."

"How long are you planning on staying in L.A.?" Reshay asked.

"Until I know my sister is willing to forgive me."

"I think you're asking for too much too soon. But, you're forgetting about one thing."

"What is that?" Jackie asked.

"Aunt Maurine has been lied to for over thirty years. She just may wild out on you as soon as she sees you."

"Shay, please. Maurine is a Christian. She's not going to do anything but quote the bible at me."

"I don't know mom. If I were her I would try to knock your lights out."

"That's enough. Go home and pack. I'll take care of everything with your flight."

Chapter Thirteen

Janitta stood beside Maurine. "It sure is great to see you and Mr. Johnson together after all these years. It gives me hope that there's still true love in this world," Janitta said.

Maurine rolled her eyes. "I don't think they've given my baby a good bath. You men need to get out of here so I can take care of her. We all know she takes a million baths everyday just to relax."

"It's funny you say that because she and I were laughing about that not too long ago." Davion replied.

"Do you need us to bring anything back?" Jimmie asked holding the door open before leaving.

"No." Maurine filled the small basin with warm water.

Davion followed Jimmie out the door. "Mr. Johnson, what's going on?" he asked.

"Not to be rude, but, son, everyone will find out in due time." Jimmie walked toward the waiting room.

"Okay." Davion nodded his head.

Jimmie retrieved his vibrating cell phone from his pocket. "Hello," he answered.

"Reshay and I are here. Where should we go?" Jackie asked.

"Meet me at 1221 North Conrad Avenue. I'm on my way." He ended his call. "Davion, I need the key to Carrie's house." Jimmie pushed the button on the elevator.

Davion fiddled with his key ring. "Sure, I had a company clean everything up. You should be okay there."

"Thank you. I need you to bring everyone over after your visit with Carrie."

"Yes, sir." He sat in the waiting room for ten minutes thinking about what was about to go down until Maurine motioned for him to come back inside. "Is the coast clear?" he asked.

"Coast is clear, honey." Maurine straightened the fresh new sheets on Carrie's bed.

"Where's Dad?" Stephanie asked.

Davion played with MaTaysha's curly hair. "He went to Carrie's house. He said I needed to take you guys there whenever we leave here."

"Yes, I know." Maurine kissed Carrie and stoked the side of her face.

"Mom, what's going on?" Stephanie asked.

"Patience, honey." She doted over Carrie.

"Mom, could you look at me for a second and tell me what the problem is with you and dad?" Stephanie demanded.

"When I said patience, I meant don't ask me again."

Taysha jumped on the bed. "Mommy you opened your eyes. I missed you so much."

"No, Taysha, you have to be careful with your mommy" Maurine placed Taysha back on her feet on the floor.

"I want to hug her, Granny." Taysha frowned.

"I know you do, but mommy is very sore. You have to be gentle with her."

"Yes, ma'am."Taysha sat by the window.

"Hey, sis, I love you." Stephanie bent over and whispered in Carrie's ear.

"I... am... so happy... to see... you," Carrie groggily replied.

Davion held her hand. "Hi, honey."

"I... didn't... know... you... were here."

"I've been here every day. I'm not going anywhere."

"Ok… ay."

Davion leaned over to kiss her cheek. "Don't talk too much Carebear."

A nurse knocked on the door. "Hi everyone, I'm sorry but visiting hours are over. Only one person can stay if you'd like."

"Not this time but thank you. Please take care of her while we're away. Don't hesitate to call if we need to come back."

"We have all your numbers." She chauffeured the family out the tiny hospital room.

Davion pushed the button on the elevator. "Well, I guess we need to head over to Carrie's house."

"Can't be soon enough," Stephanie replied.

"This is where we part ways. I'll talk to you all tomorrow," Janitta said stepping out of the elevator.

"What time will you be here?" Davion asked.

"I have a few photo sessions in the morning but I shouldn't take too long. I may get here around noon." She opened the door to her car.

Stephanie ensured Taysha was buckled in. "Carrie is so lucky to have a friend like Janitta. I never had a friend like that."

"Stephanie, you've had tons of friends. What are you talking about?" Davion said driving away from the hospital.

"I've had tons of acquaintances. I don't have any true friends," Stephanie explained.

"I can't see how that could be. You're a great person with an even greater heart," Davion replied.

"I can be your true friend Aunt Stephanie," Taysha said.

"Aww, I love you little lady." Stephanie hugged Taysha.

"I love you too," Taysha giggled.

"Move out the way man," Davion screamed and blew his horn at the other drivers.

"Why are you rushing?" Stephanie asked.

"No rush, just hate when I'm behind slow drivers," Davion replied jetting down the highway.

"You young people are always in such a rush. What you are rushing into it beyond me," Maurine said.

"You're right Mrs. Johnson." Davion exited the highway.

"Mom, you're a little snappy. This isn't like you," Stephanie observed.

"Don't psychoanalyze me Stephanie. I know what you're doing."

"I thought I was the only one who noticed you tend to do that in random conversation. You think there is an underlying emotion behind everything people say. Then you analyze it to death," Davion laughed.

"Hey, don't attack me for caring about you people," Stephanie laughed.

Davion parked in the horseshoe driveway. "I'm just giving you a hard time."

Maurine rushed through the door. "Jackie, what the hell are you doing in my daughter's house?"

"I'm here because I love you and I'm so sorry for what I did." Jackie walked toward Maurine.

"Don't put your hands on me sister. However, I do agree that you are a sorry sad person. I never would have imagined my own sister would do something like this to me. I was so busy watching out for those tramps in the street that it never crossed my mind the tramp was right under my nose. Boy, family is something."

"It wasn't like that, Maurine. It's hard to explain but I never meant to cause this kind of confusion. I guess my happiness over shadowed your pain." Jackie backed away.

"I could never look at you the same. Helen tried to warn me so many times about you," Maurine replied.

"What would Helen know about anything? She couldn't even hold on to her own husband after two kids herself."

Maurine slapped Jackie. "Don't you ever talk about our sister that way. Especially when she is not here to defend herself anymore. You didn't even have the class to show up at her funeral."

Stephanie interjected, "mom, what is this all about?"

"Jimmie, tell your daughter what's going on." Maurine sat down.

"Darling, why don't you have a seat next to your mother and I will explain."

Davion bolted for the door. "I think I'd better go. I'll be back later."

"No, you're a part of this family. It's okay for you to stay," Maurine replied.

"I appreciate that, but I would much rather go. I should let you guys have some privacy. Really, I'm okay. I'll call to check on everyone later." He walked out the door.

Reshay ran beside Davion. "Hey, could I hang with you? I'm sorry mom, but I don't want to be a part of this."

"Shay, like it or not this involves you more than anyone else," Jimmie said.

"Please, respect my decision." She closed the door.

Jimmie grabbed Jackie's arm. "Let her go. Give her time."

Jackie sat next to Maurine. "I don't want you to hate me. Please, take into consideration I'm still your sister."

"Have you lost your mind?" Maurine stood.

"What is that supposed to mean?" Jackie asked.

"It means you can't have a relationship with my husband. Have a child with him. Then expect me to remain the same with you."

Stephanie covered her open mouth with both her hands in disbelief.

"Give me a chance to be a better sister to you. I lost my way. You're supposed to be a Christian. You have to forgive me." Jackie pleaded.

"I don't have to share a relationship with you to forgive you Jackie. I love you and I will pray for you. You should be ashamed of yourself," Maurine replied.

"This isn't the proudest moment in my life but I can't take it back. Tell me what I can do to make it right, please," Jackie replied.

Maurine placed her finger on Jackie's forehead. "Let it go right now. The point of point of you all being here is so Jimmie could speak his peace. I can't stand the sight of either of you." Maurine walked away.

"Don't run Maurine. We have a lot to talk about," Jimmie replied.

Maurine put her hand on her hip. "What else do we need to talk about?"

"What do I need to do in order to help our marriage survive this?" Jimmie asked.

"I need some time to myself. Can you handle that?" Maurine said walking out of the house.

Jimmie followed Maurine. "I know you'll always feel a certain way about me. Please don't throw our marriage away."

"You don't need to talk to me about throwing away anything. I never had anything to throw away. You're such a joke as a man and a husband."

Jimmie touched Maurine's arm. "Calm down, honey. Please lower your voice."

"You're asking me to be someone I'm not. You had a relationship with my sister. Not a fling, but a relationship. I get sick to my stomach when I think about all the times you were intimate with her and then came home to me like nothing happened."

"As long as you hold on to those thoughts, we'll never make it. Could you at least go to counseling with me before you let it all go?"

"Is that supposed to magically fix our problems?" Maurine replied.

"No, but it could help us to find our way."

"I need to get away from you and Jackie." Maurine sat on the white-ironed, patio chair on the porch.

Stephanie stood beside Jimmie. "Dad, it may be best to give her space right now. Pushing could only make things worse."

"Stay in your place. I'm talking to your mother right now." He held his hand up to quiet his daughter.

"Give her space," Stephanie screamed.

Jackie charged toward Stephanie. "Watch your tone, little girl."

"You really need to back the fuck off, Jackie." Stephanie put her finger in Jackie's face.

"Oh, so you no longer refer to me as your aunt?"

"You're lucky I don't refer to you as the backstabbing bitch you are," Stephanie yelled.

"That's not called for. You may not be happy about things but you will show your aunt respect," Jimmie interjected.

Maurine walked away while everyone was arguing.

"Maurine, don't try to sneak away. We're sisters; we need to talk about this," Jackie said.

"I'm leaving because if I stay I'm afraid of what I'd do to you."

Stephanie held Maurine's hand. "Come on, let's go for a walk," she said.

Maurine followed Stephanie away from the house hand in hand. "So, what are you going to do?" Stephanie asked.

"Honey, when you get this far in a marriage, you never believe something like this would happen."

"What gets me is out of all the people Dad could've been with he chose your sister. I can't believe Daddy could do something so scandalous," Stephanie replied.

"He's a man, honey. I don't know why I thought my husband would be any different."

"This is pretty mind blowing."

"You don't need to hold this against your Dad. None of this involves you or your sister."

"Dad lied to all of us. How could you expect me to be okay with that?" Stephanie asked.

"Baby, I've tried to protect you girls from all things that may harm you. This will only make us stronger and as long as we stick together we will get through this. Nothing, and I mean nothing, will ever tear us apart. So, hold your head up, my dear girl. Dry your tears because everything will be okay in time."

"I never would have thought Dad would have it in him to be so deceitful and carry on with a lie for so many years."

"Believe me, I had a feeling things weren't so perfect. But, I had you girls and I did what I thought was in the best interest of my kids. I didn't want you girls to grow up without your father."

"Why should you dismiss your happiness for the sake of ours mom?" Stephanie replied.

"I stand by my decision to this day and I wouldn't change it for anything."

"I understand mom. Let's head back so we can get some sleep." Stephanie kissed Maurine's cheek.

***

Reshay sat alone, tapping her fingers on the arm of the chair in the waiting room. "So now you're going to act like you don't know me, Shay?"

Reshay shrugged her shoulders. "I didn't think you would want to talk to me."

"Why not, you ran out last night and we never had a chance to talk. Did you try to pull a stunt like your mom and sleep with Davion?"

"Not in my character." Reshay brushed her hair out of her face.

"I didn't think your mom had it in her either."

"I know you're hurting right now so I'm going walk away before you piss me the hell off," Reshay replied.

"You need to check your tone and don't point your damn finger in my face like you're chastising a child because I'm very grown. You better remember who you're talking to." Stephanie stood.

"Honey, trust me. You don't want to take it there. I'm not the same little girl you used to push around. As it stands we have the same bloodline darling. Have a nice day." Reshay walked out of the waiting room.

Stephanie screamed at the passing voyeur. "What the hell are you looking at, lady? Mind your damn business."

The woman sucked her teeth. "If you weren't making a scene, I wouldn't have stopped. Learn to keep your family business in the house."

Janitta ran into the waiting room. "What was that all about?"

"Just some lady being nosey as hell," Stephanie yelled,

Janitta laughed. "You will never change. How's our girl doing this morning?"

"She's well. Everyone's in there with her. Davion called that detective to find out if anything has changed."

"Good deal. I can't believe she's already responding. God is so good. Yes, He is. Praise the Lord." Janitta waved her arms in the air.

Stephanie placed her manicured hand on Janitta's shoulder. "Hey, hey, now don't start shouting in the hospital," she joked.

"You need to find God so you can get some of that hell out of you."

"I don't have any hell in me. Where have you been all day?"

"Taking care of business," Janitta smiled.

Stephanie looked at Janitta's short black dress and silver heels. "I'm loving the look. Head to toe honey."

"Thank you. I bought this dress the last time I went shopping with Carrie."

"It's really good to see how much you care about Carrie. Did you hear about Dad and Aunt Jackie?" Stephanie asked.

"No, what's going on?" Janitta turned toward Stephanie.

"Hold on to your seat. We found out last night that Dad and Jackie have been having this sick affair for years, and the kicker is Reshay is not our cousin but our sister."

Janitta gasped. "No, are you serious?"

"I wish I were joking." Stephanie tapped her feet.

"I can't believe Mr. Johnson would do something like that. He's a man of integrity."

"He's no different than any other man. He just knew how to keep his shit out of sight, out of mind."

Janitta hit Stephanie's leg. "Watch your mouth. How's your mom taking all this?"

"Better than I would be right about now. She's being nicer than I would be, too. I would have tried to break Jackie's fucking neck." She mimicked with her hands how she would succeed in her actions.

"We all know what you would've done. Furthermore, I'm surprised you haven't tried," Janitta laughed.

"I almost did back at Carrie's house. She better be happy Dad stepped in with his snake ass."

Jimmie sped around the corner. "How can you sit here and talk about me this way?"

Stephanie crossed her legs. "I'm going to ask you nicely to remove your finger out of my face."

"Yes, I messed up. I'm human. I'm going to make mistakes. Have you forgotten about all the things I've done for you and how I've always been there for our family," Jimmie said.

"So what, that was your responsibility. You lived a lifelong lie and that makes you the biggest coward in my book," Stephanie screamed.

Jimmie smacked Stephanie's face. "You need to stay in a child's place. I don't care how old you are. I love you and

I don't deserve this. I never meant to hurt anyone. I acted selfishly and I was only thinking of myself, but I've always been a damn good father to you."

Stephanie rubbed her red cheek. "Don't you ever put your hands on me again, old man." She ran down the hallway.

"I've never hit any of my children before. I don't know what to do. I've lost my family." He fell into the gray chair and cried into his trembling hands.

Janitta rubbed his back in a consoling motion. "Mr. Johnson, we all make mistakes. People handle their emotions in different ways. You're just going to have to work hard to regain everyone's trust again. Stephanie's hurting and acting out because she placed you on a pedestal. I'll be praying for you. I'm going to go check on her." Janitta stood.

"Thank you, Janitta."

Chapter Fourteen

Stephanie sat outside in the dark smoking a cigarette.

"That's a nasty habit I didn't know you had," said Janitta walking towards her.

Stephanie held the cigarette up. "I've been smoking for years. I tried to stop several times, but to no avail. I'm sorry you had to witness all that drama with my dad."

"Would you like to talk about it?" Janitta asked.

"Nope, I don't have anything else to say." Stephanie lit another cigarette while still holding onto the other one.

"Don't you think you're being a little hard on your father? He's human and as humans we tend to make mistakes Stephanie."

She blew a puff of smoke into the air. "That's something else I don't understand. Why does everyone keep calling a thirty year affair a mistake," Stephanie replied.

"He's your father and an excellent one I might add. Maybe to a certain extent he was a lousy husband, but you shouldn't forget about everything he's done for you. If my memory serves me right, wasn't it your dad who gave you blood when you had those problems with your anemia. You were so afraid you would get sick with anyone else's blood."

Stephanie put out her cigarette. "I should've been afraid to take his blood with all the creeping he's been doing with Jackie."

"Stop talking like that. It's totally inappropriate. I love you guys as if you were my family and it's killing me to see this going on," Janitta cried.

"I appreciate you trying to comfort me and fix things, but to hell with him. I don't want to talk about it anymore. I'm going to see my sister, and then I'll be going home as soon as I can get a flight out."

"Don't leave things like this Stephanie. You will regret it. It's not too late to make things right."

Stephanie held the door open to the hospital. "Are you coming or what?"

"Sure, I'm coming."

Stephanie stood by the door. "Don't look at me like that. Janitta, put yourself in my shoes."

"I wish I could, but when I was eight years old, my dad passed away of a heart attack. There's no getting that back." The ladies walked to the elevator to return to the divided family.

Stephanie rubbed Janitta's back. "I'm sorry, but I've always thought of my dad as my hero. What am I supposed to do now? How am I supposed to look at him the same way?" They stepped out of the elevator and headed to Carrie's room.

"Just love him, Stephanie," Janitta replied.

"You're right," They heard a lot of commotion from the waiting room.

"What's going on," Janitta ran to the group of people.

"Clear the area. Get him on the gurney," A doctor yelled.

Stephanie cried, "Dad. What happened to him?"

A nurse held Stephanie away from the working doctors and nurses. "Ma'am, you need to stay back and allow the doctor to help him."

"I don't understand. He was fine a second ago."

"Please, just allow the medical staff to help him."

"Where are they taking him?" Stephanie cried.

Janitta ran to her side. "I'm sure he will be fine. The doctors are very good here."

"This is my fault isn't it?" Stephanie cried.

"If you would've kept your mouth shut, he wouldn't have passed out." Jackie pushed Stephanie's shoulder.

"Get the hell away from me Jackie. If it wasn't for you our family wouldn't be in this mess." Stephanie pounded Jackie with her closed fist.

"Don't stand there and watch, Janitta. Get her off of me," Jackie begged.

"I should let her beat you for what you did," Janitta said pulling Stephanie away.

"Davion, why are you looking like you just saw a ghost. You can't be surprised this fight happened with the stunt Jackie pulled," Stephanie said tugging on her shirt.

"It's Mr. Johnson. He had another stroke. I just asked the nurse what was going on and she told me he's been taken to an operating room."

"Oh, no," Janitta gasped.

Stephanie yelled, "Don't think for one second I'm done with you, Jackie."

"I'm still your aunt and you're going to respect me."

Janitta placed her arm across Jackie's chest. "Back the hell off. I've had enough of you today." She pinned Jackie to the wall and turned to Stephanie. "Go with Davion to get your mother."

"You need to stay out of this and mind your own business." Jackie said trying to free herself of Janitta's grasp.

Janitta moved her arm to Jackie's throat. "I may appear to be a pushover to you, but don't test me. I love this family and I think you're the lowest form of rat shit for all the pain you've caused them. I'm only going to ask you once to keep your mouth shut. If you're a smart woman, you will catch the first flight out and go home."

"I'm not going anywhere. I love that man and I'll be here as long as he's here."

"Keep your distance while the immediate family is around and keep your mouth shut. No one wants to hear anything you have to say. Do you understand me?" Janitta released her hold.

Jackie rubbed her neck and grabbed her black purse from the floor. "I will not be shut out. I'm a part of this family, too."

"Not today, not this week, or for however long it takes. For the time being, it would be in the best interest of everyone for you to remain at a distance."

"Damn all of you if I lose my Jimmie and don't have the chance to say good-bye." She pointed at the rest of the family walking down the hallway.

Janitta whispered in Davion's ear. "While you guys are here, I'll go sit with Carrie."

"Please, don't leave me alone with them. I don't know what to say. "Davion replied.

"I'm just a few steps away if you need me, now go check on Mrs. Johnson and Stephanie. They need someone right now. It's time to man up."

Davion nodded. "Mrs. Johnson, Stephanie, is there anything I can do?"

Maurine clutched her worn Bible with tears in her eyes. "He's gone, Davion. Baby, he's gone." She lowered her head and sobbed.

"I'm so sorry for your loss." Davion embraced the two sobbing women.

Stephanie stepped back. "I shouldn't have said the things I said to him. I should've known better. Dad was sick."

"Stop it. You were upset. We were all upset. None of this is your fault." Maurine grabbed her hand.

"Then why do I feel so bad, Mom," Stephanie asked.

"Baby, listen to me. I wasn't so nice myself. With all that he and Jackie had thrown on us, we reacted as anyone in our position would have reacted. It doesn't change how much I love him."

Davion rocked Maurine in his arms. "Everything's going to be okay."

"Thank you, baby," she whispered.

Stephanie looked at Maurine. "I will never forget the last conversation I had with my Dad. I think it would be best for me to go and deal with this on my own."

"Please don't go Stephanie. What will I tell your sister?"

"You have Davion and Janitta. You don't need me. I love you guys." Stephanie disappeared down the hall.

Maurine buried her face into Davion's chest and sobbed. "I don't know what to do."

"Be strong, Mrs. Johnson. I know you're a woman of faith. There is nothing you can't get through."

"There's only so much one person can take. Ever since we got the call about Carrie, everything's been falling apart."

"Mrs. Johnson, bad things happen in life, but we have to learn to take the good with the bad. God is going to get you through this and make you stronger. There's no way he will forsake you."

Maurine fell on her knees and stretched her arms to the sky. "I call on you, Heavenly Father, to give me strength to get through this. Lord, make me stronger for my children. In the name of Jesus, I thank you for all you've done for my family and I know there's a blessing in this storm. I pray for my daughters and I pray you show my husband mercy. I thank you in Jesus name. Amen."

Davion repeated, "Amen."

Maurine rose with more strength and faith than she'd had in all her years. She would need that strength to give Carrie the news. The two strolled down the hallway to Carrie's room. "Janitta, I really appreciate you being here, but do you think you could take Taysha out for a moment."

Janitta shook her head. "Taysha how about we go to the cafeteria and see what yummy food we can pig out on," she said

Carrie looked into each of their faces. "Why does everyone look so sad? The doctors hasn't said anything about me has he?" she asked, holding her chest.

Maurine sat on the side of the hospital bed. "Baby, a lot has happened. I will tell you about it all but I need you to stay calm and be as strong as I know you can be," Maurine explained.

"Go ahead, I'm listening."

"Some things happened and I guess it was too much for your dad to handle. He had another stroke today."

Carrie gasped. "Is he okay? Where is he?" She struggled to get out of the hospital bed.

"Honey no, lay down. Listen to me. He didn't make it this time."

"I don't believe you," Carrie frowned.

"I know it's hard to accept, honey." Maurine cried.

"Was he home alone when this happened mom?" Carrie asked.

"No, he was here."

"Dad was here. In L.A?" Carrie held her pillow tight in her arms.

"Yes, as soon as he got the news you were in the hospital, he came right away."

"Dad wasn't in any condition to travel."

"I know, honey, but you know your dad. Anytime something went on with you girls, he was always there and this time was no different."

"So, in other words. If I wasn't in the hospital Dad would be okay." She sobbed.

"I'm going to tell you the same thing I told your sister. We can't control God's will. It was time for Him to call his child home. Your dad was tired and he needed to rest. For so many years, he was the backbone of this family. He made sure you and your sister got through school. He gave you values and raised you with integrity. He has played so many roles. We need to pull together and be here for one another now."

"Mom, this is so messed up. Where is Stephanie?" Carrie asked.

"She's dealing with this the best she can on her own."

"Where is she, Mom? You know how reckless Stephanie can get. I don't want her to get herself into any trouble. That's the last thing we need. Problems on top of problems," she cried.

Davion stood. "Hey, no, stop crying baby. I'll find Stephanie and make sure she's okay. Don't get all worked up. I understand this is a lot to deal with, but you have to remember you're still recovering."

"Thank you, Davion. Tell her I need her here with me," Carrie replied waving goodbye.

Maurine kissed Carrie, leaving her alone for a while. She slowly strolled down the hallway and sat beside Janitta and Taysha who were eating candy bars. "Well, girls, I guess this is the end of an era for me."

"No, Mrs. Johnson, it's a new chapter in your life. You're going to be fine because you're surrounded by so many people who love you. We will help you through this." Janitta consoled Maurine.

Maurine noticed a tall man nearing the waiting area. "Who is that? He looks so familiar."

"Yes, he does but I can't see his face."

"Oh, it's Jason," Maurine said snapping her finger.

Jason removed his black shades and ball cap and leaned over to hug Maurine. "Hi, Mrs. Johnson, how are you doing?"

"Jason Lenom, I haven't seen you since our family reunion. You had that fast tail girl with you."

He laughed. "She was a good girl. I know it's been a while, but when I heard about what happened to Carrie I made it my priority to get here."

"How did you find out?" Maurine asked.

"My mom told me last night," he replied.

"Carrie will be so happy to see you." Maurine held his hands.

Janitta stood with her hands on her hips. "Boy, don't act like you don't know me."

"J baby! Wow you look so different."

"I lost fifty pounds and cut my hair. What do you think?"

He took Janitta's hands in his, and looked into her eyes. "I think you should be Mrs. Lenom. That's what I think."

"Boy, stop it. Where is Sherry?" she asked.

"She's home. I didn't need anyone tagging along." He knelt down. "Is this little Taysha?"

She clutched her grandmother's arm. "Hi."

Jason looked at Maurine "My goodness you're a spitting image of your mommy. So, how's my best friend doing?" He waved at Taysha as Janitta did her best to divert her attention from the heavy details of why her mother was in the hospital.

"She's talking, but she's not able to walk yet. She was shot in her stomach and she's had surgery. So far they believe they've repaired all the damages. She'll need a lot of rehabilitation to regain her strength," Maurine quickly explained.

"Who did this to her?" Jason asked.

Maurine smiled at Taysha. "It was Terrence's ex-wife. Supposedly Terrence had no idea Cynthia was planning to do this."

"Is she awake right now?" he asked.

"Her nurse just gave her medication. She's out like a light."

"I guess I'll go get settled in at my hotel. I made arrangements to stay here until Carrie's better. By the way, where's Mr. Johnson."

Maurine looked down. "I don't want to talk about that right now."

"Is everything okay?" Jason asked.

Maurine gripped the arm of her chair. "No, not at the moment."

"I understand. Janitta, where's William," Jason changed the subject.

"I have no idea. I haven't talked to him." Janitta replied with a frown.

"Sorry to hear that. Is Stephanie around?"

Janitta stood. "How about I walk you to your car."

"I agree. Hopefully people will think I have enough swag to pull a fine woman like you when they see us walking together," Jason laughed.

"Still mannish," Maurine laughed.

***

Janitta took a deep breath after her long explanation to Jason. "So, you see we're really happy that you came. This family needs all the support they can get right now."

"This is mind blowing. What the hell, man, no wonder Mrs. Johnson didn't feel like getting into all the details."

"Yeah, she's a trooper. I know everything hasn't hit her yet. I'm going to do my best to get Mr. Johnson's arrangements taken care of for her."

"Let me know if you need me for anything. Where's Davion," Jason asked.

"He's out trying to find Stephanie. Hopefully he will be back soon."

"It's not like her to leave and not tell anyone where she's going. That's totally out of her character."

"She's dealing with a lot of emotions right now. The last conversation she had with her dad was horrible. She basically told him he was no good, and by the time I got her to understand she needed to talk to him, he was gone."

"This is too much even for me to hear."

"Where will you be staying while you're in town?" Janitta asked.

"I reserved a suite at the Ritz Carlton over on Admiralty Way."

"Uh, well, if you weren't already spoken for I would've snatched you up myself. You've come a long way since we all used to get those super savings motel rooms," Janitta laughed.

"I remember that trip. That was the night you and I made love. Damn, girl if it wasn't for the distance I would've made you my wife. I still haven't gotten over you."

"Don't start stroking my ego. You know you're nowhere near ready to make anyone your wife baby."

Jason held Janitta's shaky hands. "Honestly baby I've been thinking a lot about settling down. I won't get into this today but we will soon. Tell Davion to call me on my cell or come over. I'm in suite 8006," He replied kissing Janitta.

She embraced Jason. "I'm going to hold you to that handsome."

"Make sure you do. I'll be back in a couple of hours sexy." Jason drove away.

***

Carrie woke to see her entire family in her room. "Jason, hey, what a surprise. When did you get here?" she asked.

"A few hours ago. This news scared the heck out of me," he said.

"I was scared myself. I never want to experience anything like this again."

"So, what happened," Jason asked.

"I'll tell you about it another time when my pudding isn't in the room." She smiled at Taysha gazing into her eyes.

"Well, I'm relieved to know you're doing better. I don't ever want to reunite with you under these circumstances again."

"Believe me if I could make that promise I would. Mom, what are we going to do about Dad?" Carrie asked.

"I'll arrange for him to be taken back to Washington, and I'll go from there."

"I'm going to miss my dad," Carrie cried.

"I know you will, sweetheart." Maurine patted Carrie's leg.

Davion walked in the room. "Look who I found."

"Oh Stephanie, thank God you're okay," Maurine said hugging her first born.

"I'm fine mom but Davion has something he needs do." She pointed and walked Taysha out of the room.

Davion knelt on one knee beside Carrie's bed. "I love you so much and the time without you was so unbearable for me. It has soothed my soul to have you in my life again. When you were hurt, I really saw how empty my life would be to not have you in it. Would you please accept this ring again and be my wife I promise you I'll never leave your side again. Will you marry me?" He asked.

"This is so sudden. How in the world did we go through all this just to get back to where we were? Yes, Davion, I'll marry you," she cried.

Janitta smiled. "I always knew you two would eventually find your way back together. I guess that's how you know when it's true love. Now, all you need to do is work on that divorce."

"Oh, you're too funny Janitta. Well, you keep laughing because I know something you don't know."

"What would that be?" Janitta asked.

"In due time. You will see in due time," Carrie laughed.

"Hey, where did Reshay and Jackie go. I hadn't noticed they were missing with everything that's been going on," Davion asked.

"They went home. It's better to deal with that at another time," Maurine replied.

"I know I shouldn't have done this right now since you still have a lot you need to get in order with Terrence but I couldn't wait another day. I'm sorry for my lack of better timing but when it's heavy on your heart you have to do what you have to do."

Stephanie poked her head in the room. "Is it okay to come back in now?"

"Yes, you need to hear this too. You kids never cease to amaze me. You pray and pray for someone good in your life. Then when you're blessed with that person and you don't know what to do to let that person know you love them and are happy to be with them. So, you end up splitting up. Then you go on and life happens and life is created. Then you're back like nothing happened. Well, I'm going to tell you like this. I am not having this anymore. You two obviously can't live without each other so this time you better hang on like it's nobody's business because life is so dang short it's over before you know it. Take note and love with everything you've got and love faithfully." Maurine explained and dabbed her teary eyes.

About the Author

Author Tasha Wright was born in a small Texas town in Mexia but currently reside in Dallas, Texas. Living in such a small town, she had to find ways to occupy her time, so she began to write short stories. It began as a hobby but as she allowed others to read her work, people would tell her she should publish. Her first book published was Carelessness of the Heart. She always says she hopes everyone enjoys reading her work as much as she enjoyed creating it. Her goal is to help her readers escape their world if only for a moment to enter another.

Tasha Wright

What goes around comes around, a lesson Shay learns all too well in *Karma*. Shay, a young and beautiful business student, launches into the world of drugs, sex and betrayal with a little help from her boyfriends. The first, Smooth, is a smalltime drug dealer just trying to get back in the game. After giving him her all, Shay learns just how scandalous Smooth can be.

In the process of leaving Smooth, Shay meets Diondre—the cities number one supplier. Using his charm, Diondre manages to sweep Shay off her feet. Soon, Shay finds herself caught up even deeper in the vicious drug game.

As Shay lives the privileged life of a kingpin's girl, she dreams of one day settling down. In order to have her dream, she must find her way out of the game and the abusive relationship that came along with it. Will Shay be able to break the vicious cycle she finds herself in, or Karma cut those dreams short?

Take a trip with Alexis "Cherie" Norwood in her debut novel as she walks you through the life of Marie Aili b.k.a. Bittersweet from Chicago, Illinois. Marie is an honor student in high school with aspirations to go to college. However, she has her own problems with her mentally ill mother, aging grandfather, and a selfish aunt. Her life changes when she meets up with a young hustler named Keshawn who decides Marie is the one person in the world he loves and trusts.

Keshawn is a street smart hustler that has his own problems with his mother forcing him into the game, the dangers that he encounters in the streets, and the people around him that he trusts less and less each day. After meeting Marie, he decides he wants to get out of the game so he enlists the help of Marie and her family, and asks Marie to become his safe girl. Although, Marie doesn't know what this entails she agrees to help Keshawn. This decision will flip Marie's reality upside down and catapult her into a life that she is not prepared to enter. Keshawn tries to protect Marie from the consequences of street life, but that is a promise that he can't really keep.

Will Keshawn and Marie end up together or will they succumb to the pressures of the game that threaten to tear them apart?